D0205658

The Duke

Memories and Anti-Memories of a Participant in the Repression

Enrique Medina

Translated from the Spanish by
David William Foster

Zed Books Ltd.

The Duke was first published in Spanish, under the title *El Duke*, by Editorial Galerna, Buenos Aires, Argentina, in 1976; and first published in English by Zed Books Ltd., 57 Caledonian Road, London N1 9BU, in 1985.

1st edition: Buenos Aires, November 1976.
2nd edition: Buenos Aires, December 1976.
The military government of Argentina banned the book in January 1977. The democratic government of Argentina lifted the ban on 2 January 1984.
3rd (revised and definitive) edition: Buenos Aires, February 1984.

Cover design by Henry Iles.
Printed by Cox & Wyman, Reading.

British Library Cataloguing in Publication data

Medina, Enrique
    The duke: memories and anti-memories of a participant in
    the repression.
    1. Title
    863[f]   PQ7798.23.E28

    ISBN 0-86232-409-2
         0-86232-410-6 Pbk

US Distributor
Biblio Distribution Centre, 81 Adams Drive,
New Jersey 07512, USA.

Preface

Enrique Medina (Buenos Aires, 1937–   ) has averaged at least one book every six to twelve months since he published his first novel, *Las tumbas*, in July 1972. *Las tumbas* (The Tombs) may be considered one of the most scandalous events in Argentine literary history, and it went through over 25 printings in five years; after being unavailable from 1977 to 1982, it is currently attracting the attention of a new generation of readers in Argentina, avid for a 'writing without concessions' that addresses their concerns in a society that has gyrated wildly between different political oppositions, only in recent months to enjoy such democratic freedoms that permit the sort of writing Medina proposes to offer.

Like so many first novels, *Las tumbas* is autobiographical. The title refers to the name given by internees to an infamous combination juvenile reformatory and orphanage where Medina spent his teenage years during the years of the first Peronista government. However, as several critics have noted, *Las tumbas* was more than just another insider's story about these dreary and destructive social institutions. Insisting that narrative writing in Argentina could never again treat the trashing of the individual by repressive social institutions with the euphemisms and artful evasions that frequently buffer the depiction of such institutions for well-intentioned but naive and squeamish readers, these critics have focused on Medina's unshakeable conviction that only through a 'writing without concessions' to good taste, a ' "contestatorial" writing' that reflects social violence in a rigorously faithful mirror of verbal violence will it be possible to successfully challenge those social, political, and hypocritically moral structures that trash the individual while hiding that activity, that 'process' (to use a word with multiple resonances in an Argentina that has only recently undertaken to free itself from military rule) behind a mask of civilized gentility.

As a consequence, the writing in *Las tumbas* proposes an implicit continuity between the violence of the reformatory, and controlling structures of society. The reformatory is a microcosm of the latter, and the shocking impact of Medina's language and his depiction of the nature of 'correction' behind the walls were naturally read in Argentina as an accurate image of the society they inhabited.

Censors are, one must lamentably note, reliable readers, if only by accident: banning Medina's works as immoral was certainly reasonable because they are a gesture of defiance in the face of prevalent moral hypocrisy; banning Medina's works as pornographic unquestionably made sense if pornography implies a criterion of corporal experience that has been forcibly sublimated in the interests of a more unrestrained social control; and banning Medina's works as subversive can only be seen as an accurate assessment of how they implicitly demand an attitude of defiance in the face of the comfortable myths of complacent, cynical, and self-serving tyrannical governments.

Medina's third novel, *Strip-tease*, is a 500-page tour de force that portrays Argentina's strict and repressive moral values against the backdrop of an imaginary world of seedy striptease joints and the self-defeating masturbatory fantasies they engender; fantasies that constitute the individual's only release in the social theatre he inhabits. (It should be noted that Medina's early works deal with the victims of repressive trashing in terms of man, but in his more recent works he has come to adopt more and more of a unique feminist voice; more on this below.)

Like the writers he claims to have read with attention — the Burroughs of *Naked Lunch*, the Bukowsky of *Notes of a Dirty Old Man*, the Céline of *Journey to the End of Night* or *Death on the Installment Plan* — Medina makes use of a wide array of elements usually judged to be antiliterary and in poor taste. These elements include the cliché ridden flotsam and jetsam of Western mass-culture societies, and, as repugnant as his materials are in isolation, with their emphasis on the physical and spiritual degradation of the individual in a repressive and oppressive society, his most nauseous passages are underlain by a clearly definable moralistic vision of man and by the imperative to define ethically a standard of conduct in the face of cynical and exploitative structures of power.

El Duke concerns an individual who is unable to comply with this imperative, despite the glimmerings of authentic human feelings beneath a consciousness encrusted by the slag of the interests he is obliged to serve. The novel is the pre-death interior monologue of the small-time ex-prizefighter whose ring name provides the novel's title. Silently directed to a rat that has sought refuge from the rain in the shack where the man is hiding from the unnamed death squad/mafia agents he has served, the interior monologue allows the protagonist to review the sordid details of his life, his services as a parapolice hitman, and the way in which he is now to be a victim of the unnamed agents (the latter is ironic information for the reader, since The Duke believes that he can escape their reach).

The continuous flow of monologue is interrupted by various types of narrative segments: post-death interviews with individuals associated with The Duke by newspaper reporters on the lookout for the headliner scandal; flashbacks to The Duke's rootless existence in the human cesspools of the 'Paris of the Southern Hemisphere' (Medina is a master at lacerating Argentine cultural myths); pithy sketches (at times in a pseudo-dramatic form) of the activities of The Duke and two partners who serve as paid assassins for the local Syndicate and the forces of law and order the latter overlaps with: the leader of these angels of death is a weekend painter and model father whose executions are ballet-like, gratuitous butcherings.

Any discussion of Medina's writing must inevitably deal with the question of the presentation of violence. One of the recurring motifs in his narrative is the verb *basurear*, which I have previously used in its English equivalent, 'trashing'. Medina views the common or humble individual as a victim of trashing at the hands of those who abrogate for themselves the tyrannical roles of power, whether these be political, economic, or religious. The structures and mechanisms of these roles of power treat any individual who cannot yield to their will as so much trash to be disposed of. This trashing may assume the form of economic and social exploitation, it may assume the form of degrading penal treatment (as in the case of *Las tumbas*) or it may assume the form of official government persecution, torture, and assassination, as has been repeatedly the case in Argentine history.

One of the points to be made in connection with Medina's writings is that what appears in a superficial reading of the novel to be the gratuitous representation of assault, rape, and butchering is in fact the adherence to the author's imperative that one must speak of the truths behind the façade of Argentine bourgeois gentility, forthrightly and honestly. Violence is gratuitous in Argentina, as it is in so much of Latin America. This is precisely the whole point of Medina's novel and of his writing in general. The problems he has had with the censors and other self-styled champions of the public weal is that the 'immorality' and the 'obscenity' of his fiction are that it tells the truth. Of course, so many passages of his novels could, in a reading inattentive to Latin American socio-political reality, appear to be an aggressive portrayal of violence against men, women, children. But one of the points Medina has made in his fiction concerns the weak and unprotected, so often women and children, as the ultimate scapegoat in the strangling chain of violence. His most recent novel illustrates this point well. *Con el trapo en la boca* (With a Gag in Her Mouth, 1983) is perhaps one of the most important feminist novels to have been written in Argentina, and it, too, certainly deserves to be translated from Spanish. The English-language *Buenos Aires Herald* called it a faithful depiction of a girl of the *Proceso*: the Process of National Reconstruction, that destroyed so many segments of Argentinian society in its course, among them the sense of self-worth and identity of the younger generation.

In the novel, this Process Girl, having learned well the lessons of violence taught her by society, castrates her boyfriend with a razor blade as a gesture of rebellion and revenge against the structures of macho dominance on which her society is founded. The circle of violence, of course, therefore remains unbroken, and this is exactly the problem facing a society like Argentina as it returns to democracy in the shadow of the constant threat of a reassertion of control by the military.

In more specific terms, the actual forms of violence portrayed in *El Duke* can be verified by reference to the many reports by organizations like Amnesty International. Such acts of violence, which cannot be hushed up or explained away, are an abiding feature of the death and torture squads, one of the techniques of terror and horror used to control political dissent (hence, the title of Medina's 1981 *Las muecas del miedo*, The Grimaces of Fear). The image of the man being cut up into little pieces and the image of the woman being assaulted before her child are portrayed in *El Duke* both as literally true examples of organized, officially-sanctioned violence against the Argentine citizenry and as a synthesis of the serial violence that touches not only the 'guilty' (those who have overtly incurred the wrath of the mighty) but also innocent bystander-witnesses who make the fatal mistake of not averting their gaze in time.

If one of the reasons we read literature, with its complex blend of the fictional and the documentary, of the imaginative and the testimonial, is to contemplate a heightened (but physically, if not emotionally, safe) image of the human condition, it is important for our understanding of the texture of life in areas of the world like Argentina to experience a shock of understanding that moves us, no matter how incompletely and tentatively, toward a sense of the terror experienced by Medina's Argentines. This may not be the only legitimate image of Argentina, which is, after all, a very lovely country in other respects and probably in the long run does not degrade its citizens too awfully much more than does Britain or the United States (Medina might disagree with this observation, but we are not obliged to have identical views on the subject). But it is a vision that, unfortunately, has the compelling ring of truth about it, and it is therefore for this reason that it cannot be argued away as immoral, obscene, or pornographic.

David William Foster
Arizona, 1984

Diego knew how to appreciate good boxing. Those sure movements from the waist that left the enemy gloves suspended in mid-air. That restless head, calculating beforehand where the next blow was coming from and ready to avoid it.

Few knew how to stand up in the ring like The Duke. He was more than just a 'gent'. Elegant and strong, he lent his art a presence that completely justified the nickname he had won. He was all-round: he knew how to take care of himself and he knew how to attack. According to Diego he was the best all-round boxer we had had up to then, the only one who could represent us with dignity in foreign arenas and if he took care of his personal life he could even get to be world champ! No one really believed that, but Diego did, insisting and arguing with vehemence.

Diego knew how to appreciate good boxing. He was a fanatic of The Duke's. He did not agree with Luis that 'boxing is the art of defense' or with Carlitos, for whom 'the best defense lies in attacking.' He was convinced that boxing was the art of defense plus the science of attack, and he tried to demonstrate it shadow-boxing in jest and dancing around on the tips of his toes.

The Duke's legs were in a class by themselves: they were beautiful. It's a real boon for a boxer to have long, thin legs. His form is more agile and all of his power is concentrated from the waist up. On the other hand, there are boxers with thick legs and, as a result, a bad distribution of their weight. A real disadvantage. Marciano was an exception. Robinson was the greatest, the best of all time. And his legs were long and thin, with the result that he was capable of tremendous movements. Moreover, his perfect height worked with his well-molded physique to give him half of his advantage. The rest had to come from the boxer: an aptitude for the sport, the will to win, extensive training, attention to his manager's advice, extensive training, an ordered life, extensive training.

Diego was convinced that The Duke had been struck from a very special mold, which had then been thrown away. Extensive training was the key.

Diego, Luis, and Carlitos had been going to the stadium since they were kids in the sixth grade, sometimes with their fathers, other times with their uncles or with various family members who were into boxing. And sometimes they just went alone. They usually bought general admission tickets, not only because they were cheaper, but also it was fun to join in singing and shouting until they were hoarse. Then they would spend a half hour in the bar commenting on and arguing over the details of the fight. If the fight had been won fair and square, if the judges needed glasses, if the knockout had been planned out in advance or was just the result of a lucky blow.

Diego dreamed of being a boxer and following the example set by The Duke. He was sure he could be one of the best. He came to love good boxing thanks to that marvel who could set the crowd roaring by just raising his arms.

Diego discovered The Duke that time when they were unable to go to the stadium because of his grandmother's wake. But they put the radio in the kitchen on low and learned that an unknown boxer had ko'd one of the top-ranking fighters. Who was the stylist who had taken all of the fans by surprise? No one could remember his name. The announcer had said that his fighting had the elegance of a duke.

A month later Diego went with his father to see him. Despite the draw, he was stunned by his style and by the precision with which he controlled his left jab. On the way down the stairs from the general admission section, the people could talk of nothing else but The Duke.

At the next fight the announcer just used his nickname to announce him: 'And in this corner — The Duke!' The crowds roared like on the best nights.

He and a group of fans stood around for about two hours, breathing heavy on the window of the restaurant where The Duke had gone to eat along with an entourage that couldn't stop patting him on the back. When he finally came out of the restaurant, Diego at last got The Duke to autograph a photograph he had bought outside the stadium. The pen, skipping on the glossy print, scrawled out 'The Duke' in an untutored hand. His face was still unblemished and his nose intact (the advantage of a good defense). They trailed after him until, in the next block, still accompanied by his friends, he got in a car.

For a whole week Diego bored his friends by telling them about the moments at The Duke's side. He not only showed them the autograph. He had also made up a talk he had had with his idol, and he even began to believe himself.

That autograph opened the album-scrapbook that with time would be enriched by a large quantity of clippings, interviews and photographs of all his fights.

Diego remained loyal until the last fight, when the Duke grabbed the ropes in order not to fall, his face hidden by a mask of blood. Diego, his hands hurt from gripping the wire mesh that separated the ring-side seats from general admission, could not hold back a wild cry that mixed tears and saliva.

Diego was loyal forever, until the very end.

He slept all afternoon, dreaming of the fight. More than a dream it was a nightmare. That really couldn't happen to him. He would win the title and, moreover, a long and brilliant career awaited him. He awoke with his forehead bathed in sweat and the hairs on his neck standing up. He splashed water on his face and went out for a walk. He managed to calm down. He had a sixth sense that enabled him to understand everything, and what he was understanding he didn't like at all.

The stadium was jammed and the ticket sales had exceeded all records. The police strained to keep those without tickets from sneaking in the various entrances. Halfway through the warm-up fight the only cry that could be heard was 'The Duke!' Thousands of burning throats were calling for him. He put on his red dressing gown with his name embroidered in golden yellow on the back and paced around his dressing room. He whistled, like a canary in a cage. His campaign had been arduous. They hadn't given him that chance on a silver platter — he had won it after many fights. What's more, they hadn't taken him seriously, always pairing him with those has-been tryouts, future night-watchmen or cabaret bouncers. He had arrived, with great effort. The warm-up fight was over. Don José patted him on the back and they went out into the corridor. As soon as they saw him, the whole stadium seemed to come apart with the roar of the crowd. It was a great night. He put up with the touches from those seated at the ends of the rows and mounted the stairs to the ring without showing any reaction to the frenzy that had taken hold.

It all went quickly, even though the fight lasted all the rounds, even though Don José begged to be allowed to throw in the towel, even though he was able to fool the doctor by telling him he could see perfectly well. Almost blind in one eye and the other filmed over by the blood from the brow above it, there wasn't much he could do against an adversary that had good reason to be the champ. Despite his smoking, sheer strength kept him upright through that overwhelming punishment. He did everything to get in close or to block so he could strike, but the distance proved fatal. In his corner, they did what they could to stop the blood and the swelling of both cheeks. He went on, hoping for a lucky blow that would put everything back in place like everyone knew it should be. Why, even the defender knew that that night he would have to give up the title to the one that everybody considered the real champion, give it up to The Duke. But fate had arranged things differently, and The Duke held on to the ropes so as not to fall. He was ko'd, but still standing. At heart he had the pleasure of denying his adversary seeing him humiliated. The bell rang and it was over. Shouts, clapping, crying stabbed at his ears. The fans acclaimed and congratulated him for not having cheated them in defeat, since triumph had not been possible. The fans always love losers with a sense of shame. He did not bother to raise his hands or even to await the decision. Climbing out of the ring, he remembered the nightmare. He heard Don José: 'We'll ask for a rematch.' But he knew that he had fought his last fight and that now the bell would ring open a new fight in his life, one that was very different from those he had had to face up until now.

get out of this damn hole I'm fed up with having to go next door for water and fill the barrel with the bucket that Doña Lola gave me what a great ole gal Doña Lola I'd like to be able to help her but how can I help anyone if I can't help myself yes I've got to help myself starting today tonight I guess by dark this damn rain will have stopped even if it doesn't I'll have to do it just the same I can't wait it's not decent not having anything to eat especially when you're working shit you break your butt working and all you get is a kick in the ass sure you can tell right Pepe no no you can't tell or maybe Doña Lola's right we have other lives and are born again and are transformed into others and also into animals poor Pepe luckily you hit hard and didn't suffer and that S.O.B. of an engineer wanted to be right with us the ones who were wrong because we didn't check the ropes before lowering the scaffolding of course he said fellows be careful with that pulley and by the same token I can say be careful the tub doesn't have any water in it when he already jumped from the trampoline he knew the pulley was acting up and that you had to keep checking it and patching it with wire why didn't the bastard buy a new one Pepe couldn't be undoing and redoing the wire every other minute and you get too sure of yourself and start thinking that the scaffold is part of you and that's not surprising because I already knew every inch of my rope it's hard to believe but I knew my rope and Pepe knew his but he got overconfident and he almost took me down with him what a rescue god damn I'm sure heaven warned me that's the only explanation I almost never grab the rope that time I must have been hanging on to it I felt this tingling sensation on my feet the whole body tingling something terrible to hell with the buckets of paint with the board with Pepe when you're at the eighth floor there's no escape probably not even with a parachute because there's not enough time for it to open even if Doña Lola comes over and sees me still lying here she's going to get mad but she won't really come after the fight last night she has almost a week to be mad in and me about a week to disappear from the map of the world from everywhere from this country a new life and get out of this never-ending poverty Mirna is probably going to pick up someone in the bar to get me to take notice she thinks when she goes to bed two days in a row with the same jerk I'm going to get jealous poor Mirna the truth is that lately she's been doing better and if I didn't blow it all every weekend we could get out of here and live more decently but that would mean I would have to hitch up with her in a more serious way which is what she wants she can go to hell wait and see if I'm going to get hooked up with a hole bigger than a volcano she's not as keen as she was at the start that I slap her around love me love me love me she's nuts if she thinks I love her not in my wildest dreams and the truth of the matter is who can I love the truth of the matter is that I'm not interested in loving anyone you can't make anybody love or do anything you love if you want to because after all you can't say I'm going to love or I'm not going to love you love or you don't and that's all there is to it besides I'm fed up with her whining the fool doesn't ever catch on so I'm going away I could make it with María she's young and just getting with it before someone else beats me to her I could take her with me no problem but then I realize when they are messing with me the dumb jerk acts like a fool whenever I speak to her and when I tell her to shine my shoes I bet she'll kneel down and lick them before I even get done telling her to the truth is that it's fine but the old drunk is going to get furious and he'll go to the end of the world to get even with me I'd better just forget about María I can have thirty Marías the nice part is that her name is María and she sticks with that name not like Josefa whose working name is something artsy Mirna is nice she told me I can work and earn a lot more and besides she dyed her black hair blonde and when it started growing out the black roots started to show the poor bitch thought that by threatening to cut her hair if I didn't treat her better I'd act like a lamb poor Mirna what a thrashing she got and on top of it all her face all covered with blood she had to sit still while I cut her hair imagine trying to blackmail me it looks like it's going to keep raining until tomorrow and who knows maybe I'm better off if it keeps raining because everybody'll stay at home the second thrashing came when I caught on to how she wasn't giving me all the money it's just that I'm working less now because my hair is short she told me don't you see that almost all of them like long hair she tried to give me me a line tell me that those boobs are going to notice if a whore has long or short hair when all they want to do is to bury it so go sing that song somewhere else after the second beating came the third one I can't even remember why and so you get used to it and poor Mirna ended up liking my warming her buns before putting her to work I've got to stop being a loser tonight I've got to stop being a loser tonight I'll say it over and over *again until I get up until I have the guts to do it if I believe it myself convince myself and whip myself up and everything works out okay and I forget forever the packing-house the damn packing-house ruining myself among animals and rivers of blood poor cows a dog's life at first it was hard for me to hit them right in the center of the head so the head of the hammer would knock them out cold at first I hit them anywhere and they would cry like crazy mooo mooo and they would run around in a daze so I couldn't hit them right in the center of the head poor dumb animals how many times have I put their eyes out but christ it was their own fault moving around so much if you know you're going to die it's better to die quietly rather than to fuck it up and die bit by bit the pieces of their eyes would splash on my face at first the first day it bothered me but later who the hell cares it wasn't my fault a guy's got to earn a living what the shit if the world is made that way what can I do about it it's not my fault I take care of myself amen old Ramón never misses with the hammer it's better to use finesse than only brute strength and I gave it all I had and the poor thing would fall down bellowing and I would get all nervous and then he would get serious and take my hammer and he lifted it holding it in mid-air looking right at the crazed cow maddened with pain and banging against the gate and when the cow rocked back and forth he would too and then he would swing the hammer long like a push broom and with measured force right in vital center as he used to say and buried the hammer tip in its head and plaf it fell dead away it was marvelous how it fell plaf like a sack of potatoes with a dry sound and Colorado would open the gate so the cow would roll away while he kidded me saying that if that's how I was with the women I wouldn't get their holes straight and the cow fell at his feet at his boots bathed in blood and he bent over and fastened the chain to the paw and raised it and the cow maybe it wasn't dead all the way was still bellowing whatever while he pulled it up and it swung around and banged into the one in line ahead of it all hanging in a row and the old fellow gave me back the long iron hammer and told me try again and my legs trembling I didn't know whether to grab the hammer he gave me or to keep my eye on the path the cow would follow or send it all to the devil but I had to stay there it was all I could get and my old lady was dying and I had to buy her medicine so she would die without suffering because the doctor at the hospital told me cold like I didn't have anything to do with that* woman who had no hope I don't know how long she has left but there's no saving her and he walked away and just standing there without even explaining anything to me telling me anything the bastard every damn doctor what the hell do they think they are the king of the mountain and I ran after him and I said tell me something it's my mother who do you think you are that I'm an animal tell me something give me some explanation you have the duty to tell me something and he slipped away like I was a leper and two orderlies grabbed me otherwise I'd have bashed in that ugly face with its two rosy cheeks that I still remember as if I were seeing them right now and then another doctor just like him came along and said let's go get a cup of coffee and they went off to the canteen while the two held if I run into him I'll make mincemeat of him you can bet that S.O.B. doesn't have a mother and try again Román was telling me you'll catch on the same thing happened to me I would get all nervous but only the first few days

An alarm clock goes off at 5 a.m. A married couple turns over in bed. Sorel *opens his eyes, throws back the sheet and gets up. He goes out on the balcony in his underpants, observes the city at his feet, the beauty of the morning, and takes a deep breath. He does some exercises. He starts out slowly, followed by a real workout. The milk begins to boil and runs over the edge of the pot.*

Showered and finishing knotting his tie, he eats his breakfast. With the cup in his hand he walks over to his study. He attentively examines a painting on the easel. It's a landscape. He picks up a brush and makes a few strokes on the canvas.

He opens the door to his children's room. He looks at them tenderly. His daughter has her arms around her pillow. He blows them a kiss with his fingertips and shuts the door.

He drives his car through the deserted streets until he comes to a coffee shop where he picks up Walter. *The two drive on.*

WALTER: How are your kids?

SOREL: Fine *(He smiles)*. Yesterday, the teacher gave my little girl an A in history.

They travel along the silent streets between the buildings. They stop the car. About fifty meters away is a parked car from which a man emerges. He is tall and thin, with an agreeable face despite the scars over his eyebrows and his crooked nose. The three move toward the door of a building.

They enter the elevators and push the button for the 26th floor.

S *(smiling and feigning a body blow)*: And how's the champ?

DUKE: I can't complain.

: Are you going to the fight tonight?

*ey reach their floor and are met by a friendly, balding fat man.
ey walk into a sumptuous apartment. On a small table cham-
.igne and goblets have been set out. A naked girl is sleeping in a
arge, white armchair. Bald Fat Man boasts about the night he has
spent and invites them to have a glass of champagne.*

S: Some other time, we're in a big hurry.

BFM: Fine, boys, whatever you say. It's all there.

*orel motions to Walter and the latter picks up a briefcase. He
opens it and checks its contents.*

BFM: Count it, count it! Do you think any of it's missing? It's
exactly one hundred thousand dollars, not a cent more or a
cent less. If you want, I can give you a tip for the trip, ha ha.

S *(taking the shut briefcase Walter hands him)*: No, we don't have
to count it. Don't we know you well enough? By the way,
do you know anything about Don Jorge's behaviour?

*Bald Fat Man turns pale. He walks over to the desk but Duke is
faster than he is and slams the drawer shut violently breaking Bald
Fat Man's fingers. Terror-stricken, his eyes open wider than eyes
should open. Grasping his broken hand by the wrist, he kneels
before the three men.*

BFM: I'll give you everything I've got. It's more than you can ever
guess!

*Walter swings his foot and puts the man's eye out with the toe of
his shoe.*

BFM: Owww! Please, for God's sake, spare me!

S: Lie down!

*Bald Fat Man, his face covered with blood, moves his head back
and forth.*

S: I said for you to lie down! Do it!

*Bald Fat Man backs towards the white armchair where the naked
girl is still sleeping soundly. Walter and The Duke grab hold of
him and drag him over to a picture window that looks out onto an
open space.*

13

BFM: Sorel, I promise to make you filthy rich, I swear it!

S: Smile, God loves you!

Walter *and* The Duke *suddenly heave* Bald Fat Man *against the huge picture window. The glass breaks with a dry crack.*

BFM *(falling into space)*: Ahh!

The girl shifts in the armchair and remains lost in her own world. They go down the elevator.

S: Art is the application of knowledge to the realization of an idea.

Duke *and* Walter *exchange a meaningful glance.*

For which magazine? . . . Fine . . . The truth is that I have nothing to say. It was a long time before I ever saw him again . . . No, I really don't have anything to say. He never came around here while he was well-known, while he was famous . . . We were very proud . . . Who are 'we'? We're us, the people in the neighborhood. Those who knew him as a child . . . Yes . . . He was a good kid, a little withdrawn, but very good. Yes, he lived with his mother in the same small house . . . She was away at work all day and used to take him with her, but she barely had enough for medicine, you know how it is . . . Well, yes, she died in a hospital but he was committed because he had an attack of insanity and had hurt some other children with a club . . . That was very strange, he was so good, he ran errands for the neighbors, he was a good worker. During a time, to help his mother out, he worked with a man in the neighborhood, on small jobs. You know, he mixed the cement, carried the buckets, things like that . . . Of course, everyone liked him in the neighborhood . . . No, nobody knew he had come back even the few who did see him didn't recognize him, so much time had gone by . . . Yes, he came to see me and told me — I already told the police about it, right — he told me, I don't feel well and I'm going to stick around for a few days, but don't tell anyone, ok? Since he had always been such a quiet type, ever since he was a little boy, then I did what he asked me to. I didn't ask any questions, I could just see he needed help and you consider yourself a Christian woman and you provide that help because you never know what you'll come back as in the next life . . . Yes, I believe in reincarnation . . . Well, everybody's got his own ideas . . . I respect other people's

. . . Yes, we all watched his fights in the neighborhood. Almost all the fellows and the girls in the neighborhood had his pictures in their rooms, because he always was handsome, don't you think? I loved him like a son, see . . . After so many years, both of us changed, him and me . . . When I saw him coming from way down the street, I said to myself: that's Duke . . . And I wasn't wrong . . . We had both changed quite a bit. I was very old and fat and, in spite of his smile, he was a man without any joy . . . Yes, physically we were two very different people, but it was like not even a week had gone by . . . He gave me an affectionate hug . . . He almost cried . . . He was still handsome, even if his eye was a mess . . . No, I knew nothing about his life, after he was through boxing . . . No, don't know . . . Those are things you hear, and he's not here to say they're lies . . . No, I don't know, those are things you newspapermen know about . . . You should know . . . No, I don't know anything, I already told the police . . . Of course I was happy to see him . . . Sure, he was starting to turn a little gray . . . No, he didn't go out at all. He told me not to bother him and not to tell anyone he was here . . . Of course I didn't tell anybody! What do you think?! No, I'm just telling you . . . Yes, I helped him get the light cord from a friend, from the Loyolas, they're decent, working people and they've already talked to the police . . . Look, what can I say . . . Everybody has an axe to grind . . . I don't believe what people say . . . Of course none of us believe it . . . No, we've all felt proud of Duke here in the neighborhood. Well, sure . . . No, not at all, just put Doña Lola, which is what everyone around here calls me . . .

then I got used to it and in the end I accepted it as something normal and he was right after all it is something normal you have to eat beef and in order to eat it you have to kill it and you can't give it a natural death you have to kill it like you kill in war like we kill each other pitilessly that's like what the hell then I started liking the job it suited me fine I started having muscles from so much lifting and swinging the hammer truth is that you feel great when you hit the mark it's like you're proud to do something right to kill a cow without its suffering because the truth is that when I had a bad day and missed all over the place especially when I had too much to drink it was terrible I even would miss the head and get the neck once one went crazy on me it wouldn't hold still and I hit it on the back without thinking twice what the hell the old man saw what was happening and ran over and grabbed the hammer and with that flair that I envied him for with his arms in the air and swaying like the tree tops he took care of the problem with a single blow of the hammer and the door would open and the cow would roll forward and Colorado kidding me would put it in line and going up with the cleaver in his hand he would get the odor from the beast full in the face he would open its chest carefully with class and plunging the blade in to the hilt where he knew the heart was and gushes of blood would splash all over him but since he was in full swing he would jump aside elegantly like this and everything would end up stained red we would all be stained red it was unbelievable to see how the cows would go on mooing and quivering and exuding that thick hot stench when they should be moving never again that's the way nature is old Ramón would say while he checked my swing follow through follow through bring it out clean and sometimes I would hit it right and when that happened it was a pleasure to see the cow roll down the ramp sometimes you got a bunch of skinny ones and they were more restless and backed against the walls of the pen like mad they knew that the bath they got when they came in the plant was a trick it wasn't to welcome them it was to wipe them out neatly. treacherously with premeditation and treacherously like Zezella said in his diary that guy who had raped the little girl wearing a white uniform which is a lie because the girl wasn't on her way to school and that bit about the people in the neighborhood wanting to lynch him was also a lie when they brought him around for the reconstruction of the crime truth was that they yelled jokes at him and Zezella laughed at the jokes right there between the police who were escorting him what happens is that everybody who read the diary couldn't see the child and know that she wasn't a child and that she was running after Zezella and in the end like Doña Lola says sooner or later you drop the plate washing it so much and the girl ended up and well Zezella had to end up some way and you'll just have to get used to your new life I'm not sure I wouldn't have done the same thing because truth of the matter is that the girl was great it's no different from spending the day banging cows on the head in the end I started liking it and felt something like pleasure when the tip of the hammer hit the mark it was like I felt a charge of electricity or something from the handle of the hammer from the cows brains to my hands and my whole body that was the only way to get used to it to make myself like the work and when I was able to find it a pleasure was when I beat Mirna for the first time with her it was also hard to get used to liking it but when I started really liking it we got along great in some ways I was the screw for her nut our sessions caused some uproar in the rooming house and we had to move to another we ended up thrown out of seven rooming houses it was wild like we were tourists until we got tired of always doing the same thing and she started to be a drag with the love stuff love me love me love me and I who the hell am I going to love who am I going to love if I don't even know if I loved my old lady truth is that I don't know if I ever loved anyone is that so bad or isn't it I guess if everybody talks about love it's because it must be real but to be frank nobody absolutely nobody matters to me now that nobody means anything to me and that I don't mean anything to anyone it's better to get by that's all you can do what you want with no *problems no being anyone's prisoner no wife no kids no bother when my old lady shoved off that was all I had left I shoved off with her she was the only one I always had by my side how many fine houses I got to see when I went with her to do the washing one house after another and me always hanging on to her skirts afraid of the crappy dogs they'd come around sniffing me and dogs are never wrong when they smelled me like an animal from somewhere else they would realize we had nothing to do with their masters it looks like it's raining harder and harder shit now it's started to leak over there what should I do I can get up and move the chair or I can stay here on the bed without moving because truth is tonight I'm vanishing from the face of the earth they're going to have to hunt me with war spies to find me ugh what a rat where the fuck did it come from those creeps can go through the eye of a needle like nothing damn if it isn't huge it looks like it doesn't realize I'm here on the bed what a balance it has let's hope it doesn't lose its footing or it'll drop on top of me it must have climbed the drainpipe it must have come from the house next door they must have been plugging the pipes and the poor bastards must have been dog-paddling poor thing it's cold as hell it's holding still now if I call it if I startle it what'll it do it'll run off sure enough and slip from fright and fall down on top of me better not to make any noise and let it decide what to do when it stops raining dogs' and rats' weather just think all the medical tests are done with those poor beasts and if you tried to domesticate them like a cat or a dog who knows maybe they'd be cute and nice like puppies that wake you in the morning licking your face the rat would run across the pillow and would squeak low in your ear and you'd open your eyes and see that tiny face and the wrinkled snout full of whiskers greeting you on the new day it'd be great to try to raise a rat a cat and a dog together how nice if they were friends and you could walk them in the park and the rat would be there perched so cute on the back of the dog giving the neighbor cats the finger and the three would play together I remember that in one of those fine houses where my old lady went to do the washing there was a cat and a dog that were friends they had raised them together and pity anyone would try to do anything to the cat my old lady and I would get into the city real early after a horribly long ride on the bus an old broken down bus I don't know how it could still go on the dirt roads the dust would come in through the floorboards and the* passengers would all get covered with it and I would sometimes sleep because the trip was very long and my old lady never slept she slept on the way home when she was tired out from scrubbing all day on the way in she would calmly look out of the window without ever blinking I would secretly study her I would guess how long she would stay with her head on her chest and we could go by block after block and she'd never move sometimes it scared me and then I would shake her arms and ask her what she was thinking about and she would tell me that she was looking at the houses the nice houses and I'd ask her if we'd ever have a nice house and she'd answer that she didn't know I was happy to have her hand caressing my hair and we would play at choosing a pretty house in general we agreed on one with red tile roofs of course I always rode by the windows we'd grab a seat because we got on early and right away it would fill up and people would shove old hats old bags old coats old pants old shirts tired people no smiles without talking only me sometimes wanting to talk sometimes talking to somebody but only rarely in general I would rest my chin on the window but using my arm so as not to get hurt with the bumping up and down of the bus and I would be hypnotized by the parade of houses that would go by before my eyes at times the driver would race with the train but he always lost we'd be neck and neck for a few blocks and suddenly we'd fall behind I asked my mother why didn't we use the train sometime if we went the same place and she explained to me that it'd cost more money because then we'd have to take another bus anyway the bus we were on left us where we wanted as it was we had to walk like ten blocks there was an apartment building where the doorman wouldn't let us use the elevator we had to walk up to the sixth floor using the stairs my mother wouldn't say anything to the lady of the apartment she was afraid there'd be no more work for her later I realized why the doorman was like that when I got big I went back one day when I was good and drunk she was dead then but the damn doorman wasn't there any more I would have liked to smash his face in another apartment building the lady's kids didn't like us so we'd have to wait out on the stairs until she came home from school she was a teacher and then we'd go in her kids she was ten and he was eight were playing while my mother washed they ate and then went off to school in some houses besides washing clothes she also cleaned which is what she *did where we lived they gave us a small room out back where they kept the tools and the old car tires in exchange for house cleaning she'd come home all worn out and she almost always fell asleep on the bus and missed the marvelous night scene the lights that let you see what was going on inside a house dining-rooms with people around the table those large tables that always fascinated me it's nicer to travel at night than during the day as long as you get the window seat it's like a dream I dreamed my mother didn't she slept and she'd fall against me and I'd stay still so she wouldn't wake up while the rest of us looked at each other like buzzards when*

An automobile roars through the streets with complete disregard for the pedestrians. Sorel's *driving, with* The Duke *and* Walter *in the backseat. Two girls, with tape on their mouths, are lying on the floor of the car, held down by the men's shoes; every now and then they step on their faces.* Walter's *hand reaches down and starts feeling the girls' legs. The car enters an area where there's no houses, then it enters some woods.*

SOREL: Asepsin is the group of processes for the elimination of microbes without recourse to antiseptics.

Sorel *leans against a tree, smoking a cigarette. The two men beat the girls. They rape them.*

S *(he continues to smoke, paying no attention to what is happening)*: Now maybe they'll learn that you don't doublecross Don Jorge! That jerk Newman will understand when he finds his daughters.

He walks over to the car and puts the radio on.

RADIO: Let's hear it for our players who have defended so well the prestige of our . . .

He turns the dial until he finds some classical music.
The two girls are lying next to each other on the grass.

WALTER: Come on, do what I told you to!

He hits them with his belt buckle.
One, the more frightened of the two, begins to undress the other.
The Duke is quiet, but he's paying very close attention to what the

girls are doing. Walter *kicks the more passive of the two.*

w: You, too!

The two are completely naked. Walter *hits them again and the girls start caressing each other.*

w: Come on, like you liked it!

He kicks them. The two girls, with no choice, forget about everything else and yield to each other completely.

s *(picking a wild flower and smelling it)*: A lovely aroma, I'll pick a bouquet for my sweet wife.

Four bodies blended into one.

Two pistols in two hands.

The silence of the woods is broken.

The two bodies have stopped trembling in their embrace.

Walter *takes the top off a gasoline can.* The Duke *takes time out to light a cigarette.*

The next day the newspapers carry the story of the truceless battle between elements of the international underworld. One of them carries a story on the first page about the disappearance of the two daughters of a known smuggler.

We would get there and have to go in without making any noise usually there would be the leftovers of some stew in a pot and while I ate and went to bed we slept in the same bed she would stay cleaning the whole kitchen which was large and the pile of dishes and things that the owners of the house had left when I was already falling asleep she'd get into bed and we would pray an our father a hail mary and a glory to god together and then fall right asleep a long time went by like that in winter we would go to bed with our clothes on because we we'd be freezing to death the dogs were better off because they were inside the house but we were almost right outside covered by a tin-roof shed I suppose the cold in the winter caused me to accept my aunt's invitation I wasn't wild about it but my mother insisted ratty rat don't make any noise just let me remember stay still you won't get wet there and if you move around a lot you could fall and you'll screw my life up a little and I don't want to get up until I have to when I get up from this bed it'll be the last time even if my back is killing me I'll hang on until the crucial moment I suppose that at first Don Jorge'll be mad as hell but in time he'll forgive me he always liked me and after all I have to do it he'll understand I'm sure the one who'll really have a fit is Mirna but after a while she'll hook up with someone else and forget all this Tito'll probably work her but only if Griselda doesn't get in the act I don't think she'll be bothered anyway she always put up with Tito's monkey business she knows he always comes back after leaving the other women in a mess what a strange couple they make she must be about ten years older than he is or more she sure takes care of herself with those beauty treatments shit the rat knows I'm here now hell let's see if it gets scared and jumps fuck it it can't go back unless it's a hell of an acrobat in that case I'll get it a job in a circus and make a million easy does it pay attention to daddy he knows what he's talking about easy nobody's going to touch you maybe if I pretend I don't see it christ it's looking me right in the eye what'll I do it's shifting around that's right get comfortable sweetheart it'll stop raining in a while and you can stop seeing the world and get back to your family they must miss you imagine your little kiddies all alone without mommie on this miserable rainy day and the thunder mamma mia it looks just like the sky had diarrhea so much thunder bow your little head move your little snout maybe if I talk to it they say if you talk to animals slow and friendly they stay calm as long as you're not in front of a tiger that hasn't eaten for a week and if I say ps ppss pppsss to it hah there it's moving its head hi sweetie pie by the way how are things at home a hell of a day what can you do about it you've got to take things as they come in life don't you think the bitch is nodding her head like she understood me who'd have ever thought I'd be here talking to a rat just look at how a guy can end up when he's desperate desperate hell I'm not desperate it's just a manner of speaking I'm calm real calm as calm as when I did the first job for Don Jorge in the jewelry store talk about cold blood I was surprised myself at the self-assurance we acted with of course later when I tried to go to sleep even my ass was sweating Don Jorge was thrilled you're good stock he told me good stock what will he say tomorrow first of all he's going to cuss like mad later he'll have them looking for me even under the cobblestones after about a week he'll calm down and give up and then a week later he'll acknowledge my skills and my balls as he used to say to give me courage only after about a month when he's involved in something else he'll give me as an example so long to it all I'm fed up with living in hiding too bad Negro couldn't save himself only a second more he took too long to get out of these he was the last one and the bullets caught him he fell against our legs we were already sitting down he bled all over us on the way I guess he's forgiven us for having buried him in his bloody clothes without a coffin or a service it's always the good ones who get it like Pepe up there on the scaffold but it's never an engineer they're the ones who save their skin they never take any chances just like the transit inspectors who got on like vultures checking one by one all the tickets waking up those who didn't see them coming standing there waiting for the guy to find his ticket and if he gives him the wrong ticket he hands it back like it was dirty hoping like mad that the poor bastard can't find the right ticket so he'll have to pay again you should answer these guys back and say what the fuck business is it of yours but the poor jerk acts like a jerk answers weakly and then politely goes up to the driver and comes back with the right ticket and the jerk pays whatever they tell him because we're all watching him and he sits staring at the window hoping that the inspector and his anteater snout and a patch on his head will be slowly crushed by a train when they try to pull that stuff with me I don't take it I say a hell of a job isn't it and he looks at me with hate in his eyes but doesn't say a word and I just keep looking for my ticket in the thirty-five pockets I have and he'd give anything to take an axe to me and I rub it in talking about how unfriendly people are his eyes are shooting sparks and I keep on looking for my ticket do you have one or don't you and I put on my best boob's face sure I've got one the problem is I don't remember which bastard of a pocket it's in bastard hits him like a whip and then he pretends to continue on down the aisle I'll come back look for it and I say here it is and I give him a ticket from another line while I say to him I was referring to how people must hate you this is not the right one he says to me oh well it's got to be this one and add you probably like people to hate you some guys are happy when people hate them and when they can do something mean to someone no matter how small and he moves towards me his cheeks straining with swollen purple veins giving me back the right ticket and muttering shit on you under his breath and that's just what I was waiting for to give him a right to the chin and the two passengers who weren't holding on tight went down with him and I jumped out the back door which was open I'd already checked on that I wasn't going to be dumb enough to get myself charged with hitting someone in uniform or whatever I know when I hit clean and that was one of the times that I landed it just right with force those are the small pleasures of life don't you believe it ratty my friend you look so comfy there don't worry you're okay with me if it weren't that I don't plan on getting up I'd have given you something to eat by now but never mind go dry off and after I've left this hole is all yours you can even eat the roof I don't care I have this feeling that I'll never come back here whenever I've foreseen things they've come true so my little job is going to turn out fine just like that heist *at the Voodoo how great that turned out how did I get mixed up in that ah because I'd picked up some extra money I got the idea to study radio by correspondence and they informed me that if I wanted to learn anything I'd have to go to class I don't remember how much it cost all day I would work in the herbatorium being poisoned by the herbs stuffing them in a thousand little packets thousands of herbs we would work with our noses and mouths covered by a handkerchief but first it was the job in the machine belt factory I was fine there nice people there were only a couple of us they paid me terrible of course was only an apprentice as soon as I'd turn right to the ads for apprentices there was an apprentice for you name it so I went on to painting I could hardly hold the brush but I caught on right away and would strut all over then I got in with Don Carlos what a hell of a guy Don Carlos was and I never saw him again that's what's bad about me I stop seeing anyone who helps me the problem is that I'm ashamed to go empty-handed or to have to lie about what I'm doing but I'd like to see them Don Carlos's family you might say was the first one I had Don Marcelo's was the second what a laugh I always ended up with the honorable ones Don Carlos Don Marcelo all great people with marvelous families who gave me everything and what did I amount to that's what I want to know maybe what I'm doing is fine who knows Don Carlos really showed me how to be a painter he sure was an artist he liked the job to turn out perfect nobody ever complained clients always got him new clients we worked slow but it was worth it we even liked to stand back and look at the job when we were about done we worked in houses and apartments people with apartments are usually conceited and pretentious while people who live in houses are nicer of course we made a mess shoving furniture from one room to another you had to put up with us Don Carlos was smart he liked to eat well we'd stop at noon on the dot never a minute later better even earlier and we'd go to a good restaurant in the neighborhood that he'd found out about from the newspaper vendor or a shopkeeper and we'd eat like kings he'd never worry about the bill I could eat whatever I wanted drink all the wine I'd want to even have a nice flan with cream or caramel or watchman's dessert which is jam and cheese and then a nice coffee with a name-brand cigarette he always smoked name-brand cigarettes he'd been a sailor and had a lot of friends and always got a lot of smuggled goods but at wholesale that is for pennies no more just* so he could have good whiskey and good cigarettes it was a scream to see him in the neighborhoods where we worked if there was a bad restaurant and another one that was good or only a very good one he'd always pick the very best and we'd waltz right in dressed in our work clothes of course not with our paper hats on but our hair combed neat and people'd look at us serious I'd be embarrassed like hell the first couple of times when I'd hear we were going to nice places I'd wash up fast and change clothes I'd still be embarrassed because he'd have his work clothes on he'd laugh and once when we were eating dessert he told me don't be so embarrassed to be a worker be embarrassed if you're a thief or a murderer and then he ordered cognac to go with the coffee he said it to me nonchalantly as though it weren't important and after that I never again changed my work clothes to go to a nice restaurant and

From the balcony of an apartment a little girl, her face reflecting her astonishment, is watching the patio of a neighboring house. A young man is trying to escape from The Duke *and* Walter, *who are pummeling him with their fists. They corner him, kick him, and drag him by the hair inside the house.*
The child runs and calls her mother.
Sorel *finds a pistol in a cupboard. He places it on the table.*

S: Is this the one you used?

The man, bleeding from the mouth, remains silent. They tie him to the chair, his arms securely tied to the arms of the chair. Through the window in the room, between the curtains, you can see the window of the apartment where the mother and her little girl are watching.
Sorel *realizes they are being watched.* Walter *gags the prisoner.*
Duke *puts his cigarette out in the ear of the man who is tied up; his eyes roll up so only the whites are showing.*
Sorel *looks over toward the apartment again and only sees the child.*
Walter *slides his tongue along the edge of a shiny razor.*

S: Don't stop. I'll be right back.
W *(to the prisoner)*: You're going to curse the day you were born.

Sorel *turns the corner. A beggar stretches out a hand toward him and receives a bill.*

BEGGAR: May God bless you.

Sorel *scans the fronts of the apartment buildings.*

The razor is slicing off an ear.
Sorel *steps out of the elevator, checks the letters of the apartments and rings the bell of the one marked D.*
The razor, with some difficulty, chops through a finger of one of the hands.
Mother and daughter are frightened by the ringing doorbell. They can see a man wearing dark glasses through the peep hole.

S: Telegram . . .

The mother opens the door part way. Sorel *suddenly shoves the door all the way open and the woman rolls across the floor. The telephone is off the hook. After closing the door,* Sorel *picks the receiver up.*

RECEIVER: Hello, hello madame. Answer me, please give me the address . . .

Sorel *carefully hangs up.*
The razor finishes severing the last finger from the hand, which is now a bleeding stump that struggles vainly to free itself.

W: We're in no hurry.

Sorel *holds the little girl by her hair, the pistol pointed at her small head. The mother is to one side kneeling as though she were praying.*

S: Nice view you've got here.

The razor slowly slices off the other ear.

MOTHER *(crying)*: Please, for the love of God, don't hurt my daughter! I'll do anything you want!

The razor finishes cutting the other ear off, and Walter *brandishes it triumphantly.*
Sorel's *naked legs. Mother and daughter, two women, running their tongues over the hairs, down to his toes, slobbering all over them, washing them. The man's hand caresses the woman's hair, pulled back in a bun.*

S: Loosen your hair.

She obeys, still crying, and loosens the ribbon, some bobby pins. Her hair begins to cascade down her back.

30

The prisoner's mouth is now lacking the entire upper lip, and you can see his wounded gums. His teeth are stained red with the free-flowing blood.

S *(his eyes showing ecstasy)*: Shake it free and let it fall forward!

The woman shakes her hair out in a fan that sweeps through the air.

S: That's more like it!

Walter's *hands undo the zipper to extract the prisoner's shame. The woman spreads her hair out over the man's feet.*

S *(entranced)*: Now dry them!

Walter *stretches the man's member and poises his razor along it. The woman dries* Sorel's *feet with her hair. The razor chops the prisoner's member into slices.* Sorel *withdraws from the bedroom, smoothing his jacket. The bodies of the two women are lying on the floor, each with a hole in the head where some blood trickles out.*

S *(running his finger along a piece of furniture and seeing the dust it picks up)*: Pigs!

The prisoner, bleeding profusely from the five affected areas, his head thrown forward on his chest. Sorel *walks in.*

W *(a little mad)*: He turned out to have a weak heart!
S *(looking out the window toward the apartment he has just left)*: Esthetics. That's the theory of sensitivity. The science that deals with beauty and the feelings that give rise to beauty in us.

when the ones who were already sitting down looked at me like some kind of strange bug and generally in a despective fashion I stuck my chest out and held my head high I busted more than one guy's ass this way once we got into a fight it was when we were painting the apartment of a stuck-up dame who was a knock out and it seems that Don Carlos tried to make out with her and the old gal brought him up short we worked without any enthusiasm like she was the boss and these were everyday problems and once I went through her nightstand and found a bunch of pornographic magazines and to show off I showed them to him and he said to leave them where they were but he didn't put them back he kept them and I got mad and he asked me what I wanted the magazines for unless it was to jack off he wanted to kid me because of my hard-on he thought I would be embarrassed and I told him sure what the hell I was still at that age and you're not going to tell me that you still jack off and he made a face as if to say mamma mia the upshot was that he kept the magazines and we screwed the old dame and her husband of course when she realized the magazines were gone she hated us but she couldn't get up enough nerve to ask us to return them in any case her husband could have been the one to take them I never did understand how come she didn't cheat on her husband the guy would leave in the morning and come back late when we had already left that meant he why the truth is that if I had been the husband I'd confront Don Carlos and ask him for the magazines he'd be really be embarrassed how dumb people are they get ashamed what's there to be ashamed of if after all life is short what I liked most was to wallpaper it was a finer more toney job we did some great jobs in swell homes I remember that in one *of those homes they let us eat in the kitchen and we ate like kings what wine what cream desserts and such I was still trying to get the magazines back now it makes me laugh to think that the photos were so bad and the women so ugly that I didn't know why they turned me on so much there was one fat one facing forward and sitting on a guy and she had a mask on and the guy was peeking under her arm there were a lot in which she showed up wearing a mask and in the ones where she didn't have a mask on she was looking toward the wall and at the end of the booklet there was the same poor woman alone a full-body shot smiling away they must have given her a line and told her no we won't use this one don't worry this one's just for you poor thing if she ever saw the booklet some of them were funny as hell like the guy who hadn't taken all his clothes off and his pants had fallen down but he was trying to hold them up by opening his legs another had his socks rolled down around his ankles another with a moustache held his socks up with garters metal beds and worn spreads broken-down arm-chairs walls with aging paper but I'd like to have that booklet right now just as a memento the first one I ever had was called* The New Folies *and had little rhymes under each picture I can only remember one that said she looks hesitating because she feels something penetrating and it looked like they were dancing someone in the handgun factory had lent it to me who could have said that sometime later I'd use one of those guns well that's how life is I'm the loser tonight I'm sure I've got to win once and for all the most important thing is to stay calm and to be exact to carry out point by point what you've planned and period there's no problem I'll carry the gun just for security but I won't have to use it I'm sure at best a knock on the head and there you are I'll tie him up good and when they get there the next morning I'll already be on the other side of the river and so long oolong Don Carlos's family was important in my life what neat memories I have how nice his wife was his kids the first friends I had I went to his house to eat every Sunday at noon what raviolis what meals we were quite a few let's see Don Carlos his wife she sat near the door to the kitchen he at the head their daughter she was great next to his mother the uncle alongside Don Carlos José who was a friend of the uncle on the side I on the side and at the other end Juan Carlos the eldest son who was such a good friend I wonder what ever became of him he was always so enterprising how he loved the women he was even crazier than me* he liked to get all duded up like mad whenever he saw someone wearing something special say like a white sport's coat he would stop him and ask him without batting an eye where he'd gotten it and with not so much as a by your leave he'd grab the lapel and feel the material he'd say a great jacket thanks he'd pat the guy's shoulder and off we'd go I never could buy good clothes I'd always find the cheapest clothes possible and of course I always looked it he was the one who started giving me good clothes he'd pass on to me the things that had gotten too small for him because later he got to be huge I remember one linen jacket that I was ashamed to wear because all I had was a pair of wool winter pants and once when it was too hot I decided to wear it to a party they were giving there were some great girls there and we stayed almost the whole day and what with the food and the wine everyone started relaxing and taking off their jackets and ties and the only jerk who kept his coat on was me they all made fun of me saying that I wanted to show off I pretended to go along I couldn't take my coat off because my shirt had been sewn in the back I also remember a gray jacket and god knows what else what I liked the most was an overcoat that was just like new I had to shorten the sleeves and the length I did it myself at the rooming house being real careful and it turned out great I used it a long time even when things started going well for me with Mirna I still was wearing it I was really very proud of it where did it end up ah in the Peruvian's boarding house I gave it to their son I think it was the first time I gave any of my own clothes away he was happy to get it what's the rat scratching away at it's making a lot of noise or it just seems so what with the rain it's hard to be sure about the sound she's quiet now she must feel safe here poor beast to have to be always dashing about it's not her fault she's a rat if she's in the world there must be a reason if she did have some purpose she wouldn't be here what could her purpose be perhaps so we'll be clean and not let ourselves go Don Carlos's wife was a great gal she never let me leave without a little package with a nice slice of pie Don Juan's wife another Don nothing but Dons it's just that I was still a kid still a bit afraid and I respected the people who helped me Don Juan sold false whiskey he made it himself I helped him I met him at a time when I wanted to skip out I wanted to get away no matter how I was fed up like now I was convinced that it'd be better for me elsewhere and I would wander around the port area what I mean I was working around the port I *was selling lots the hell and gone and they had assigned me to the port area it was one of the greatest times in my life I met thousands of people every kind race color station I never sold a single lot on Sunday we all had an assigned place each one waiting for his possible clientele to stick them with a lot and I was the only one who ended up paying of all the ones I had visited not a single one bothered to show up christ why would they come if they couldn't even afford to buy a pair of shoes I went on out anyway avoiding the group chief's long face the guy wouldn't stand for one of his men not making a hit the fact of the matter was that at headquarters there was a board where each of the group was listed just like in a championship match with the names of the chiefs of each group at the top and everyone was proud to see his group win and not so great to end up at the bottom our group usually did fine all the guys sold like mad they were aces at talking with people and snaring them I think my problem was ending up with them I think if I had gotten in with a more modest group I could have stood out a bit they all scared me off specially when the chief who was a nice old souse dark-skinned kinky-haired with a wrinkled blue striped suit a dirty tie you could spot a mile away it had been tied once and that once had been like a thousand years ago so I'd take the bus around reading police novels while the other guys were telling the poor devils what a fabulous buy they were getting and it was too bad they didn't have enough money themselves they would buy a lot others would say they'd bought one because they knew they'd found out don't breathe a word to anyone I overheard it behind a door that they were going to put in a special freeway that was going to go right by there and who knows what else the truth is that when you got out there it was the end of the world you could see scattered cabins for thousands of yards there were no electric lines the road was only dirt and the buses went by every blue moon it was a riot to see the lines the salesmen would use to convince the jerks how high up it was one of the more important tricks keep in mind that this is a high zone and the poor guy what'd he know about what a high zone meant what it means is that it doesn't flood it's not like the port where you get southeasterly storms while here it's high and the guy would think but the river must be millions of miles away from here look the ground as dry as a whore's tit and a real seasoned salesman would turn around and tell them always in secret that these lots the ones over there the ones near the road right on the* corner those ones had been bought by movie actors and he'd rattle off the names of the ones everyone was talking about the methods must have been the right ones because a lot of people bought while in the meantime I'd go for a walk and enjoy the sun there was one time just once because all of the salesmen exaggerate and say they make it with all the women they sell to there was this one time I scored I was kicking the dirt around thinking what a lovely thing a sunny day is when the dame old Pericles had snared walked up to me and started talking the other salesmen gave me a look that'd kill you the dame asked me to give her the good points about the place and I did my spiel like all the rest but I could see she was so poor that I started to ask her where she worked and how many were in her family which is what we had to find out anyway to see if they really could afford it or not and she told me that the truth was it'd be a huge sacrifice for her to make the downpayment and the monthly payment together and then the next monthly payment right away I told her to take care of her mom and just to stay in the rooming house until some guy came along who'd marry her and never to buy in this place because it was a swindle and usually we got by on just the first payments or just the first one we'd wear the people down just so they'd

again, he tries hard, and this time it comes, everything stored away in his stomach rises expectantly, seeking a way out. Out his mouth and out his nose too. He feels like his neck is about to come off too. He feels as though all the garbage in his body will never cease pouring out, even when his eyes lend their cavities so that the purging will be more complete. He's crying because of the effort required by the vomiting. He thinks it's all over. But he's wrong. It's like an interminable waterfall that contracts his already empty stomach. Through his tears he can see the toilet filled with a rainbow of guck and foam. Yet another attack. He makes it through it. He bends over close so that nothing's left. So his mind'll be good and clear. The last attack comes. He opens his mouth as wide as he can. It seems to him that his guts want to spill out as though they were mad at him. But no more vomiting. Nothing's left. Nothing. Only waiting. For what? He straightens up. Just like The Duke should. Always elegant, with a unique style, incomparable, inimitable. The best. Everyone knows it. He dries the tears with a handkerchief and looks up at the ceiling. This does him good. It alleviates the headache a bit. The stitches in the right side of his forehead. What a laugh, if they were to see him crying. Him. The Duke. Him who's never been ko'd. With his trembling legs embracing a filthy toilet and holding himself up against the tiles. It would be a tragedy for a journalist to see him, the story they'd write. Like the time he got into a fight with the owner of the Voodoo Cabaret. How they played that one up. He shakes his head. He tries to control himself, to pull himself together. He doesn't want to end up on his hands and knees and . . . He flushed the toilet. He cleaned some spots off his clothes, gargled some water, wet his face and hair, combed his hair, straightened his tie, threw his shoulders back, and walked out of the bathroom. You should never back down in front of these pimps. He noticed that the billiard balls were set up on the farthest table. That was so he wouldn't bother the peaceful clients who came in to kill some time. He pretended not to notice and chose a good cue. He made sure it was straight and grasped it firmly with three fingers, and his thumb and index finger forming a nice round zero he let the tip of the cue slide forward. He was great on the green-felt table, almost as good as he was in the ring. He liked to play for pleasure and not for money. He liked to play alone because it calmed him, tuned his game and perfected it in the pleasure of being better not competing. It even seemed that the green of the pad calmed him.

'Heh, Shorty, bring me a sandwich and a glass of wine!'

Somebody put a record on. Music also soothed him. It made him remember agreeable, pleasant things, and it made him forget the things he didn't like. Although there were times when there was no way to forget that damn lame cat. He jabbed the cue furiously whenever he remembered that cat, that damn cat that appeared in his life. From the very beginning. He lost track of the caroms. He was a boy and the only thing he had to his name was that lame, frightened, flea-bitten cat not worth a damn. His friends had let it in. They had baited him and he fell for it like a greenhorn. Sure, just like a greenhorn — he didn't know his way around yet.

'Come on, take a chance. After all, that cat's no use to you at all.'

The bastards laughed in his face. They didn't say a thing, but it was clear that if he'd said no he'd look like a sissy. And he could never do that. He gave in. Even though he knew that he was all that dirty and foul-smelling lame cat had in the world. It even ate when he ate. He gave in even though he was thinking that he would never again feel its warm little body rubbing against his legs. He was a dumb kid. When they started to tie him up he wanted to tell them all to go to hell and he didn't care what they thought, but nobody was going to touch a hair of his lame, dirty cat, and much less tie him on the train tracks with his head on the rail so they could see how the train cut it off. You could hear it coming in the distance. The lame cat thought that, like always, they were just playing around to pass the time. When he saw how tight the knots were and that they kept him from moving around at all, he got nervous and tried to get away by biting at the knots, but he couldn't because they were choking him. He looked at his friend to find out what was going on. But his friend wouldn't look at him and was drawing pictures in the dirt with a stick. First he meowed softly as if to say he was sorry to be a bother. He meowed so that his friend would see he couldn't get free by himself. That they had tied him down so tightly to the tracks that there was no way he could get free. Then he meowed louder, in a more insistent way. Two or three meows in a row. He tried to tell them that his neck could feel the vibration of the track. Now. He meowed louder and longer. Yet his friend didn't hear him. But the others did. They were paying close attention. Perhaps they were his friends and would let him go at the last minute. Perhaps his friend had never been his friend. The vibration of the track was more intense. The lame and foul-smelling cat arched himself as much as he could, straining the muscles of his paws, perhaps if he could get one knot undone the others would loosen as well. But it was no use. He realized there wasn't enough time. That the vibration of the tracks had gotten as strong as it would. He knew this because together with his friend they would sit and watch the train that went into town, while he would scratch his head and cause him to close his eyes he would talk soft to him. He cried convulsively. The kids jumped up and down with their arms in the air, and some of them started throwing stones that hit his head. He saw, he saw his friend staring at him with his eyes shining with tears. Then he grew calm. He realized that his friend would help him to stand this last crucial instant. He stopped meowing and withstood stoically the blows of the other kids' stones. The vibration wouldn't get any stronger now. It became a part of the sound of the locomotive and the breathing of all the passengers the train was carrying. He relaxed and waited peacefully because he hadn't lost his friend, because when his neck started burning he clearly heard, above the infernal din, the shouts of his friend:

'Kitty!'

'What are you saying?'

'Oh, nothing. This cue needs chalking.'

'Here's your sandwich and the wine.'

'Thanks.'

And he went on counting up the caroms, racking them with elegance and mastery like nobody else could make those marble balls roll. But at times he would strike hard and abruptly, hitting to destroy, and the ball would shoot, sway, not like a ball but like a bullet, like the head of a lame and foul-smelling cat. It sliced off just like the others thought it would. Cleanly. It rolled along the grade. And he was sure the cat at the final moment said 'So long, pal.' Of course, he'd liked to kill them. They were all frightened when he grabbed the stick. Not one of them got away. The train wasn't out of sight before he was smashing the heads of all of them. The four all bloody. Their faces full of fear. Now they weren't jumping up and down with joy because the cat couldn't get free, no now they couldn't understand what was going on, they couldn't understand the velocity of that unstoppable stick which was bashing in their heads, knocking their teeth out, breaking the leg of one of them. The blow was too hard and the ball jumped the edge. He picked it up. He went over to the table and ate the sandwich. He finished the wine and continued to hit hard with the cue. Alone, at the only one of the twenty tables in use.

pay something to just get them to sign and then since almost no one could keep up the rhythm of the payments they would give up and lose the plot and all the money they had paid in if anyone made a stink they would give him back a small amount so he wouldn't create a scandal but the same piece of land ended up being sold god knows how many times so this gal falls for it one day just because she's good on the way back and on top of it I lost money because the amount I had set aside for coffee and cigarettes the next day went for the hotel room going out there with the clients was great all of the salesmen talking nonstop and offering everybody cigarettes and the clients tense like a betrayed heart coming back it depended on how it had gone now no one passed around cigarettes and the salesmen read newspapers or old magazines and the suckers who had fallen for it had their jaws hanging down to the ground anyway it was one of my best jobs I'd get to the cafe early and ask for my cup of coffee and milk I'd set my briefcase down and look around the small square the briefcase changed my life I changed social classes I stopped being a rat and became an employee I say an employee because since I had to wear street clothes and a tie it puts you in another class and besides no one knew what I had inside of course that's where I kept the maps of the plots of land and piles of payment plans but also not always it's where I kept my sandwich it could be a steak sandwich or a ham and cheese and no mistake that sandwich was my reserve because the truth of the matter is I worked like a madman if by work you mean visit people and talk them up I swear it was one of my best jobs I met a lot of people good bad so-so I say the sandwich was my reserve because I met so many people that I knew more or less where I could freeload at any time of the day that is where they could invite me to have lunch where a nice snack where a couple of good mates with cookies where a good glass of sherry where if I was really lucky a nice early meal because by that time of the day I'd be fed up with wandering around the port and whoretown once one of them who had her right foot in a cast asked me about the briefcase and I told her they were papers for my job she didn't believe me and along with a couple of others they grabbed my briefcase out of my hands and discovered the maps and I just about ended up selling them a couple of pieces of land the truth is I probably could have sold them some but I couldn't bring myself to be persuasive because I felt bad doing them in they were always so good to me the one I'd have liked to screw was fat Isabel but it was around that time I didn't have anything to do I'd play with the kids in the piles of sand or stroll on the bridge I was nuts about the view there was something magic about that bridge because I couldn't miss a day crossing it except rainy days of course and I'd see all the slum apartments and I'd think that I knew almost all their occupants with their problems all kinds of family problems or money ones or jealous love or cheating lovers or crimes yes once there was a crime of passion as they call it in the newspapers a man was found one morning with a knife buried in the center of his chest they said it had split his heart evrybody said he was quite a womanizer and had it coming to him because he was dumb enough to talk a lot and in a bar he blabbed about a very pretty woman who was bad off in her marriage her husband couldn't get it up one of those things that happen like everybody said quite a bit of time afterwards when the case had already been closed they never found the murderer the pretty woman's husband had been the executioner and he had forgiven his wife because he couldn't blame her for nature but he killed her lover as not much of a man for not respecting a woman's secret the story was neat so it seemed to me at the time and still does just out of curiosity I went over to the apartment building to meet the woman but she was always shut up inside with her husband the hangman as they secretly called him in the neighbourhood many times I stood guard to see her when she went to the store but I never did see her I even started to believe that it was all a pack of lies neighborhood legends but Don Juan assured me that it was the truth what happened the guy's mother did the shopping usually and she rarely went out only when she was sure no one could see

43

her Don Juan lived in the same apartment building on the ground floor and he used his dining room for adulterating whiskey we became friends right away because we were both fans of the same soccer team the truth is that soccer doesn't mean a thing to me but it was a way to get on with my potential clients I always agreed with them in principle sometimes I would disagree with them just so they wouldn't catch on to how I was pretending to agree with them and so we could have some sort of friendly argument Don Juan really liked the mysterious woman too but more than just like her he was in love with her he was always praising her faithfulness toward her husband to me and her dedication defending the husband according to him he had allowed her to know what love is like since he couldn't himself but unfortunately the experiment failed and the loudmouth paid dearly for his lack of discretion Don Juan was real friendly and he would invite me every now and then to eat but he always told me never to come early in the evening say not until around seven o'clock that intrigued me a bit not too much that is I respected his wishes until one day I got there around four o'clock and found him pissed off he only opened the door a crack and asked me between his clenched teeth what I wanted finally he let me in and I found his table covered with bottles of whiskey all opened and without labels and other kinds of alcohol cheaper ones that had nothing to do with whiskey he made me swear to keep my trap shut and so that's how he let me in on the business I was a big help to him because he claimed I was a reliable guy he taught me the trade and I learned how to mix the batches it surprised me that you could get a whiskey taste out of such a mishmash of drinks but he always did of course there was always a lot of water involved but in the end the mixture tasted exactly like whiskey the adulteration was done on a large scale since sailor friends provided him with packs of labels and tops for the bottles I remember we used to put the tops on with a thick rubber ring that would bruise my fingers at least it left them all red he had quite a respectable clientele and supplied all the downtown bars with me in the business he expanded his trade and we had to work like the devil we got some new accounts and we billed them all we would transport the bottles in large attaché cases or in a cardboard suitcase with room enough for ten bottles we were paid on the spot as in all undercover deals and we earned quite a bit my cut was large if you realize that until that time the most I ever had in cash was just enough for bus fare and a pack of cigarettes now and then from that time on I had enough dough to eat a decent dinner some evenings and to smoke contraband cigarettes which was Don Juan's second enterprise we made relatively little with the cigarettes at least in terms of the whiskey christ all this thunder and lightening it gets worse by the minute but the cigarettes were good and we carted box after box all around the city I was kind of proud of this work because when I'd be out on the town and see the boobs buying contraband cigarettes in the places I'd supplied I felt a bit of satisfaction with myself how great it is for an entire neighborhood to stay silent about a crime not one soul said a word a real sign of understanding what's most important is to act calmly I'm real sure about this job it won't be necessary to fire a shot at the most a knock on the head and then so long oolong let them turn the greyhounds loose after me if they want I'll be far away by then and singing serenades what's the matter mousey pal what do I mean mousey rat because you're all grown up you're restless you won't stay still in one corner stop running around on the pole careful or you'll fall down on top of me and then we won't be friends anymore careful I'll soon vanish into thin air and you'll be queen and lady of these walls you can even eat the nails be my guest make sure you leave no trace of your friend who's chatting away what a bunch of cuckoos the land salesmen were one was studying to be an actor another spent his time reading mystery novels a dame who amused herself selling land because her husband ran around on her and was never at home and at least she kept busy another a drunk not worth saving another a queer trying to get into the bedrooms of the guys who lived alone he was even willing to change the payment plans but believe it or not he was the one who sold the most someone else with a spotted face at first the truth is he made me sick but in time you got used to it and no longer even noticed it running around all day familiarizing myself with every crack in the sidewalk every newspaper vendor every waiter every baker just that dame and none of the others ever she said okay I'll go look at those pieces of land at least no one got to her until one day I looked her in the eye and got lucky and so she said yes while looking me back in the eye I'll go out there with the kids but just to get out a little just to get out from between these walls and this humidity and she dried her hands on her apron and on Sunday I was all happy not sitting around the square just reading the newspaper waiting for all the clients to come along and get on the bus someone to shout let's go that Sunday I tucked the newspaper under my arm fixed myself up spiffy the others all kidded me and the dame and her kids she had a bandana on her head and the little girl had two short braids that stuck out and a smile brighter than the sun and on the way out the dame told me she felt funny because the last time she had gone out was to a movie more than a year ago and we didn't talk much only what was necessary I liked her taut taut skin and her slanty eyes that looked through to my guts she was telling me something about it was time for me to give up this work and when all the others were working their tails off to snare their clients I grabbed her by the hand so she could jump over a small rise and it thrilled me she let me go right away and caressed the little boy and girl she told me without any emotion since he left I swore that my children would never suffer as long as I was alive that's when her eyes got red and damp and I realized I'd have to leave this job that I had finished a chapter we went back in silence the two kids happy looking out of the window showing their mother the pretty houses just like I was doing rat ratty you know that

Sorel *is deeply engrossed, painting. He's copying a landscape from a postcard. He examines his work with great pride. He answers the telephone. It's a new job. There's enough time. But he's got to start thinking about it right now. They speak in code. It's night.* Sorel's *auto rolls down a long road flanked by pines.* Walter *and* The Duke *are with him. They do not speak. The radio is playing a musical medley of hit songs.* Walter *breaks the silence:*

'We're like the three brave men . . . Do you remember the three brave men? You don't? How strange. They were three cowboys, one, the youngest, looked just like you think he would. Another was the clown of the trio, and the third was a kindly old duffer. I never missed a single one of their movies. They used to do serials. One with Black Eagle. Don't you remember Black Eagle? He was an Indian who solved everything with his fists, and they sure made a lot of noise . . . Now they wouldn't be worth a damn. The three brave men would, because they used revolvers.'

They arrive at a country house with all the exterior lights out. They get out of the car and walk carefully around the house. They find lights on in the back. From a distance they can see people seated around a table. There's music coming from the house. There's a German shepherd. They enter the yard. The dog runs up to Sorel *growling, but he puts a bullet through him with the gun, which has a silencer. They peek through the windows. The little girl says she heard a moan. The whole family stops to listen, and they turn the radio off. Only the sound of the trees swaying in the wind. The*

47

parents say it's nothing, but the child's face takes on a serious look and she calls to the dog.

'Captain!'

Silence. She gets up, runs to the door, opens it, and a large hand grabs her and covers her mouth. They go in. The father moves toward them and asks them to let the girl go. The older daughter runs over to embrace her. Walter *leers at her lasciviously while he yanks the phone from the wall. The father confronts them boldly:*

'What do you want?'

Sorel *stares at him for a moment. Suddenly he knocks him to the ground with a single blow.*

'How dare you even ask! What do we want?! Do you think we're stupid?! You know damn well what we want! Where's the shipment, the stuff, the drugs? Huh? That's what we want. All we're looking for is a dumb doublecrosser. I don't know if he's somewhere in this house. What do you think?'
'I don't know what you mean.'

The Duke *takes out a gun and points it at the head of the child who's still holding on to her sister. The father asks* Sorel *to go into the next room with him.* Walter *and* The Duke *sit down to wait.* Walter *can't take his eyes off the girl, who attempts to avoid his gaze.*

'Heh, you're cute.'

The two men return. Sorel *speaks to* Walter.

'Tell Don Jorge that it's all taken care of.'
'How am I going to tell him if I pulled the telephone line out?'
'Then we'll tell him in person.'
'And these guys? While we're gone they could call the police.'
'You're right.'
'Besides, they've behaved poorly. They're bad examples, right?'
'Exactly.'
'And sometimes so people understand, you've got to punish them, isn't that so?'
'That's so.'

At that very moment the mother succeeds in slowly opening a drawer. Her husband sees what she is doing and tries to distract the men.

'Why don't we all sit down and try to straighten this out? A glass of wine mi . . .'

There's a hiss and the mother falls mortally wounded. Walter *lays the gun across his knees. The husband runs to aid his wife, and* Walter's *gun hisses twice more. One dead body falls on top of the other. The two girls scream hysterically, and* The Duke *and* Walter *hit them hard to make them shut up, pistol-whipping them.* The Duke *goes out.* Sorel *starts to trash everything in sight, the stereo, the TV, he kicks over the chairs, knocks the bookcase down, takes down modern paintings and studies them before smashing them to bits.* Walter *drags the girl over to an armchair and shoves her down. She tries to scream, and he hits her with his fist. He tears her clothes off and sodomizes her, covering her head with a pillow.* Sorel *stops to rest a bit, and sees* Walter *in action.* 'Beast,' *he mutters through his teeth and goes back to wrecking things. The little girl comes to and sees her dead parents and her broken sister. She screams and heads for the door.* Sorel *catches up with her, grabs her by the hair, puts the barrel of his gun to her head and fires. The child falls at his feet.* The Duke *enters with two drums and spreads the liquid around strategically while* Walter *closes his hands tightly around the girl's neck, killing her. They leave the scene, tossing lighted matches after them. The flames begin the purification. The entire house is purified. They climb into the car.* Sorel *admires the flames.*

'Such a pity . . . they seemed like a nice family.'

I think the first thing we have to settle is the money he won. You know how in cases like this someone starts to talk and talk without knowing anything, and then when you want to stop the rumor it's too late. Well, I can assure you that if it weren't for the horse races, he could have lived, not without working of course, but at least comfortably for the rest of his life. There's Don Juan who's my witness. What people forget is that on what you take in you have to pay a thousand things in addition, like city taxes and . . . well, I'm not going to list them all for you, it'd take up a whole page . . . Publicity expenses and so on . . . I think in life we all have a chance, and if we let it go by it's only our own fault. Don't you think so? It's so easy to blame everyone else. Look, you know I don't have anything against The Duke. We were in business together, and if I went in on it, I can assure you he did too. In any case, there are the papers like the word of God, right? As I was saying, I have nothing against him, but you know that, as the tango says, the chickens always come home to roost . . . What can I tell you? You are what you are, you can't help it . . . Because with all the chances he had — hah, I wish I'd had half of them. Anyway, I won't deny that I'm proud of the fact that he was one of my men, but . . . Take a look at this ring. See?! He gave it to me, don't you get it? He wasn't so bad after all . . . It's just that, damn it, I don't know, life is so rotten . . . Do you know that I wanted to make him a trainer? Nobody knows that, see. I told him, be a trainer and you're home free. But he ignored me. He took care of himself, and . . . that's how he ended up. It's sad, believe me if I tell you it's sad for me. What? Don José? Look, the truth of the matter is that he disappeared from the face of the earth. No one knows if he's in the sticks or out of the country, I haven't any idea. I told him to hang around and make me a new Duke, but he ignored me, who knows the hell why, right? He was mighty proud of his Duke, said there'd never be another like him . . . Yeh, sure. No, I won't say he was bad. What I can't buy is that he thinks there'll never be anyone else like him or even better . . . If everybody thought like that, the human race'd never get any better. I think he lacked a bit of initiative. In the ring he was everything, but outside of it he left a lot to be desired. You catch my drift? Bad company. Cheap women. Why even go into it if it's the same old story, right? Nothing new under the sun, as the saying goes. Perhaps in time I'll name one of the dressing rooms after him, you know? It's all gossip, but as the saying goes, where there's fire . . . I understand that toward the end he was always drunk. Anyway . . . But as to doing something bad . . . I wouldn't want to have to pay like he did. They say when you're on the top of the heap you don't have to do it the hard way. Well, I guess I'll be going . . . Oh, by the way, I almost forgot. In about a month I've got a gem of a kid making his debut. He's a tiger, lacks a bit of polish is all, too bad I don't have Don José around. Give him a break, take my word for it. I'm trying to come up with a name for him. Who knows, maybe I'll call him The Count. Sounds nice, The Count, don't you think? Yeh, I know, I know, the nickname's got to come from the spectators. And who am I, aren't I a spectator too? Don't forget that we know how to guide the public.

you're not so ugly you look sleepy of course with this rain what can you do you've got to hang in there and hope things'll straighten out what do you think about my little job don't you think that it'll turn out fine huh you're still young kid you can be good Don José told me another guy they always surrounded me with guys Don José was a good guy perhaps the one who got the best out of me The Duke what do you think ratty rat don't run off stay still that's right nice and quiet I like you to stay here with me I'm sure I could train you I can see you're hungry I'm sorry I haven't the energy to get up to get you something to eat other than ceiling boards the taste they must have truth is I love to see you running around from one place to the other along the beam I only want to ask you not to fall off okay cause then I'd have to jump up and that'd break my spell you know that when I've got a job to do I spend all day in bed even though my back hurts I'll turn over fine there I'm facing the horizontal slats of this wall what a sad light why couldn't they have put a stronger one in misers I'd like to see the look on Don Jorge's face when he finds out I got the jump on him he's going to want to croak traitor traitor he'll insult everyone right and left and that damn Mocho'll tell him between his teeth it was his right-hand man poor Don Jorge he must be around seventy now probably older than that what an enviable will of iron a real bull what an example truth is it makes me a little sorry to have to screw him but if I don't I'll never get anywhere that's not true ratty rat that if you move your whiskers I have no choice but to do it I've barely got ten years left to really live then the season of death sets in aches and pains scorn old age the humiliation of life sooner or later you end up on your knees exhausted so much running running for what fine so

52

after tonight there'll be a new life waiting for me I'll take advantage of the few decent years left me I'll have to take care of myself with the drinking and smoking Mocho'll end up boss after Don Jorge dies I've got to get out before Don Jorge dies because the others'll just shove me to one side and I'll be screwed it's the only way I have no choice I've got to make a move tonight and hope Don Jorge understands and forgives me after all I was a real boon to him a good long time that's not so rat stop making a noise I want to finish telling you my life's story I was talking about the dame, yeh a great dame extraordinary buns how they jiggled beneath her dress after cruising that area so much I had made friends with some great fellows what neat guys what's happened to them I can't even remember their names come on with us Lungo said to me he led the pack we'll leave in about a week there's a lot of dough in it you don't have to think about it come along and the fact of the matter is I didn't doubt it a bit I knew that they didn't have to convince me much I'd beat it too that whole week I didn't see the dame the afternoon of the day before we left I went over to the apartments and since she was always washing the kids were in the doorway playing with some other kids she wasn't surprised to hear that I was off the next day real calm she repeated the act of drying her hands on her apron and went to the kitchen except for the old lady in the room next door no one else was in the building she made coffee and told me to sit down and when I was seated she drew close and touched my forehead with her damp hand I didn't like her hands they were rough and had large veins and once again she got to me and I went with her to the small and cold bedroom like a dumb kid she undressed me and laid me down and made love to me after I got dressed I gave her a goodbye kiss and she caressed my face like she was blind for a long time then she drew the covers over and turned over as I was leaving granma was eating a cracker and I went up and gave her a kiss on the lips take care of yourself she told me and took a drink of cold tea from her tin mug outside the kids were still playing with other children when I gave each of them a kiss they smiled and kept on playing I don't think I had ever felt so lowdown and mean and cowardly in my life as at that moment I have only four cigarettes left I'll have to ration them so they last me until nightfall damn cigarettes it's your fault I lost the chance I could really have been The Duke if my lungs hadn't given out on me and of course I was on the cigarette from childhood the true stamp of an imbecile is what Don Carlos always said never trust anyone who smokes they are weak false sneaky down-trodden instead of pulling forward they pull back and by the same token there's nothing more stupid than smoking it's true because swallowing smoke just to blow it out again is no big deal rather it's plain crazy and on top of it I added the bottle how could I not blow it all so we duded out like we were off to war we bought boots canteens cowboy pants thick hats earmuffs and even a hunting knife with a stamped leather sheath we all met real early at the station and started off full of joy singing like a bunch of lost drunks we kind of just set off we'd been told that they couldn't draw up the contracts in the capital that we had to be there and the rumors were grand and the least they said was that you could pick the dollars up from the streets and with just this idea we hugged the train during the trip we were already planning deals and corpora-tions of all kinds some would return and set up a business others would get married and buy a house someone else would travel the only one who had no plans was me what was my plan I'd ask myself and the answer was very simple I was getting away that was all that mattered just simply that I was bailing out and I didn't know where to I didn't know if I was leaving one place or if I was arriving someplace else or if I was doing both things at the same time as soon as we got there we felt the first blow to the chin we hadn't even finished getting our luggage down when Lungo and Petiso were talking excitedly with someone called Flaco a real messy type who was telling them the straight truth about how things really were first of all the dollars were not lying around on the ground nor anywhere else because they paid with regular money second you should've insisted on a contract before coming because if you didn't already have one they would pay you what-ever they wanted to and there was nothing to do but to grab what you could he had been there for two months and was ready to get out any day all you can do is to work with the dealers he told us it's worth it because you work a half a month or a month and they pay very well of course you really have to sweat for twenty-four hours a day the majority was ready to go back on the same train but since there was none we all went to a bar to think things through Lungo said since we were already there we should stay a couple of days even if it was only to see what are we going to see someone else said this is just a bunch of shit in the end it was decided to look into the possibilities with a dealer who might show up that same night we slept in the station some in the men's room and some in the waiting room even our guts froze in the morning it was pretty to see the city stretched out at our feet the station was at a high point we walked down the main avenue we looked like rustlers strolling down the street moreover we'd said we weren't going to shave until we worked our stay out we ordered coffee with milk in one of the bars and we drank it along with what was left of the stale bread baloney and cheese from our trip we agreed with Flaco to make a try with one of the dealers who needed people while we was looking for him we walked around the pretty white town but we only just saw the oil wells when we came to the water we saw something we were surprised to see the poor little penguins completely black from the oil it was incredible that these poor buggers could survive with their pores all plugged up from all that black oil there was no sea to speak of it was an enormous puddle of petroleum that had left the shoreline all black with last night's high tide we were surprised to see the beach was full of stones at noon we met Flaco and if we wanted to we could go see the dealer he was a fat short man very ruddy with a German face we weren't wrong he was German alright he spoke to us in his babble in a rather bossy way if we wanted some of the action that's the way it was and if we didn't so long because he couldn't stand around and waste his time we asked him to meet us in a bar at a specific time so we could all talk it over he agreed and that's what we did the bar was an infernal din some of the guys wanted to tell the German where to get off others gave in while some said it was only a month the upshot was that we were split half wanted to go back and let the rest of us try it for a month we talked to the German again and he said it wouldn't work with just five men it was either all of us or none we all started yelling in front of the German who without thinking twice joined right in and ended up agreeing to higher wages in return for longer hours and those opposed quieted down the truth is that for a month Saturdays and Sundays included and all day long what he was offering was worth it I can't remember how much he said it was he said we should vote on it and the majority would decide and we won by three votes we agreed that we would be at the station the next day and he'd pick us up with the tools since we were staying that night of course we all went to the cathouse anyway if we'd wanted to go somewhere else it would have been impossible since there wasn't

even a movie theater we had to wait because they took appoint-
ments it was all very organized you went into kind of a gallery with
large flagstones on the floor where it was as cold as hell with a little
stove in the corner we sat down on the benches that ran all down
one wall the women were sitting opposite it was just like a
neighborhood dance you nodded and she nodded too and then
someone went up to her and spoke two words hi how are you she
mentioned the price and someone on the other side of a teller's
cage gave you a receipt and you took that over to one side where an
attendant made you show the head and gave you a jar to fill when
the guy went away I had to fill Flaco's too because he forgot and
already peed before coming in we turned in the jars nice and full
and they examined them and let us go in behind the one who had
taken our money down a hall where our beloved one was waiting
for us with her timed love I entered the little room where she bided
her time with her clothes there were some pictures candles laurel
branches and a red light on the nightstand first she asked me for the
receipt and then she was sweet as she could be for those fifteen
minutes

Sorel *continues painting his landscape. He observes his work attentively. He applies the brush strokes with great care, using a traditional palette. His daughter enters, gives him a kiss and tells him that she is going to the movies with some girl friends. He tells her to be careful who she goes out with. One of the friends comes in and says that they're going to see a love story. The two leave. They say goodbye to her mother. They walk two blocks and climb into a car where two boys kiss them passionately.*

The three are riding the subway. Although there are few people, they cluster together at various points in the car, near the doors. A man in his fifties is leaning against a very attractive woman. The stations go by and they strike up a conversation, when he has to get off. Seeing the chance for a conquest, he decides to stay on. The car starts to empty. Sorel, Walter *and* The Duke *are near the door but separated from each other. The man and woman sit down to converse more at ease.* Sorel, *with a newspaper, sits down across from them. The trip continues until the car is almost empty. Only the couple, three men, and an old man and his wife remain. The man is smoking patiently while his wife vents her cares by shouting and waving a finger under his nose.* Sorel *makes a sign to the beautiful woman and she says she's got to get off; the man will go with her. She walks toward the door where* Walter *and* The Duke *are standing. The subway is midway between stations.* Walter *and* The Duke *push open the doors and* Sorel *shoves the man so violently that he slams against the wall of the tunnel, falling to the tracks still clutching his briefcase. The elderly couple are paralyzed. The beautiful woman turns on*

Sorel: *she didn't realize they were going to kill him, but he doesn't even look at her. The subway reaches the station. They leave the train. Before exiting,* Walter *goes up to the old man and addresses him in a harsh voice:*

'Damn it, can't you read? It's against the law to smoke in the subway.'

are you there ratty or have you left don't abandon me ratty friend
wait till I've gone I need you to wish me luck ah so you're still there
that's a pretty comfortable place because the piece of tin siding
forms a trough and that makes a wall for you and protects you a bit
from the cold what's Mirna up to just think I'll never see her again
never again if heaven helps me tonight it looks like the rain is
letting up it's all the same whether it rains a lot or a little I'll go into
action anyway the German came to see us early it was a large truck
covered with an old piece of canvas full of holes we went bumping
off because the driver was a dolt we couldn't say goodbye to the
city the dark kept us from seeing it Petiso kept on sleeping on the
trip the dirt came into the truck he said we were in open country
after a long stretch we reached a rather big adobe house that was
dispensary hotel restaurant police station town hall bar and god
knows what all else they put us in two enormously long rooms they
looked like hospital wards we changed our clothes and then back
on the truck we went farther and farther into nowhere we had left
the plains behind and now we were crossing through an area of
low mountains they looked more like high hills in the distance you
could see a series of curves that rose and fell when we were already
scared because we had no idea where we were going the truck
stopped we had to dig so deep by so wide for seven kilometers I
think that's right a kilometer is four blocks yes seven kilometers is
what the German said to us they threw the shovels and picks to us
and before we knew it the truck pulled away the German shouted
to us that the faster we got the job done the better our pay would be
the dirt caused us to cough for a few interminable minutes abso-
lutely no one said a word it was hard to believe that they had gone

off and left us like that Petiso was the first to throw the shovel in the air and to protest furiously against us for deceiving him and what would we do now Flaco was the only one who said nothing when we took a short rest for our throats he was the first to strike with his pick some thought it was a joke but he kept on when he saw that the ground was already loose he let go of the pick and grabbed the shovel we could tell he really knew how to use these tools Lungo was next and then me slowly the others joined in cursing and swearing and uttering fierce oaths against every living thing the ground was hard and you had to know how to hold the tools otherwise your hands would get red this was the least you could expect quite a few had to use their handkerchiefs and others had to break the blisters that were making us feel right at home in this no man's land if it had started to rain all of the sudden we would have had no place to take cover this business was for the birds and if the German and the driver had an accident who would know we'd been dumped off there at least we knew in which direction we had to dig the ditch so you could suppose that there was something over there we didn't get very far that day we stopped to rest every little bit you can bet it was real work and not like spending the whole day walking around with my briefcase under my arm we had some harsh words because some pretended to be worn out and left us idiots working finally Lungo's idea prevailed that since we were all in the game you had to play it out and finish once and for all earn some good money and get out of what was turning into a hell for us it looks like the rain has gone on vacation we all need to rest in this life my dear I feel a tingling all over my body on the back of my neck and on my forehead it's nice to feel the warmth of the bed at midday we took the sandwiches out and the bottles of wine to get our strength back we were digging away for hours each one with his own thoughts all you could hear were the sounds of the tools striking the ground no one could answer for himself at that point and some were practically asleep from fatigue the wreck on wheels appeared and we jumped in like desperate men as though it were a log in the middle of the ocean the driver was alone Lungo and I rode in the cabin so we could talk with the ox but we could get not a thing out of him he was just doing a job that's all if you guys want to earn money you'll just have to break your back and in the least amount of time possible if you take a long time the earnings are minimal it's all up to you we reached the enormous adobe house and washed up in a tub we pumped so much water that the owner came out to complain that we were going to ruin her pump we ate a really spicey stew and went right to bed because starting the next morning they would come for us at 5 a.m. but first there was some arguing in which Petiso demanded everyone's solidarity with the idea of bailing out and going back home where everything was easier and more comfortable he was all alone in this because most of us were already sound asleep while we were having a breakfast of goat's milk the truck arrived this time he wasn't alone there were three other guys from the neighboring country they were to be our companions really great companions although they were drunk all day long really drunk with a lost look god knows where from as far as working went they were the best and they outdid us by a hundred to one their arrival was a good thing for us because it spurred us on and we tried to make headway if we had been left alone you can bet we'd probably be only halfway done a couple of days later a few more arrived and the work was more bearable when you all suffer together the pain is easier to bear believe it or not we got the job done we would stop to take a look at all we had done we couldn't believe our eyes it didn't seem possible we'd had the strength to dig such enormous ditches finally they brought the pipes which seemed to me seven meters long I don't know how many inches wide something like the circle formed by your two arms when you hold hands the trucks spread them out one by one along the ditch and we had to clamp them with a kind of gigantic pliers larger than a man and then drop them into the ditch we were civilizing that no man's land we were happy because we felt like soldiers building the first fort in this world through those pipes there would flow not the liquid that had brought us there in search of big money no the damn petroleum would not flow through those enormous pipes rather something much more important water we were so excited that we tried to leave our mark wherever possible and so we wrote messages on the pipes that only the worms would read Kilroy was here on such and such a date digging ditches and later positioning the water lines Petiso was bitter and all he would write was s.o.b. German and all the words he knew I remember that in the positioning of the pipes the friends that had arrived after us would pick them up with one hand one on each end but we had to do it all together otherwise we couldn't even budge them and they would lower their arm and grab the edge with

61

their one hand and lift them up like nothing Flaco said it was the wine I guess he was defending a personal point of view there was only a little left to do we were happy because we had accomplished something we had never dreamed of and the exercise had given us some new muscles we had even lost some weight around the waist toward the end we had grown used to the work the only thing that bugged was the bad meat we had to eat every day we'd razz Gorda about it she was the owner saying she should try to vary our diet but the best she would do was different forms of stew I liked to walk in those plains when the wind was strong you had to walk leaning forward you couldn't walk upright your head at least had to be thrust half a meter down to your feet that was the only way you could keep your balance when the wind was in your face and when it was at your back you had to lean back like nothing as though a bed were there to catch you tenderly and it was a pleasurable cold but what was nicest was the sky ashy not even a painter could imagine it would be worth it to go there just to paint the sky or to photograph it it was like you could reach out and touch it the stars are altogether different and stand out more with everything a more vibrant color the sky in town is crappy in comparison what do you think about all this ratty rat ps ppss pppsss huh ratty how about some wine it's good how about it it'll stimulate you and do you good and take away the suffering in your soul I'll breathe deep at times it's like I couldn't breathe I've got to smoke less otherwise I'll end up digging my own grave right ratty rat don't you want just a sip damn I got my collar wet it's this bad habit I have of drinking in bed I have time for the little job after all the boat leaves much later and by the time they find out I'll be safe the only thing that bothers me is to have to betray poor old Don Jorge why do I say poor if he's always had a good life he had a few bad moments but when all is said and done I think he's gotten the best end of it on the other hand I always got in on things when it was too late even though Don Jorge would always tell me you're in your prime in your prime in your prime why is age always such a factor why is being old so humiliating why does a time come when you can't stand on your own two feet and you need others perhaps because nature is wise so that the haughtiest and those who run over others realize their mistakes and pay in the end but there are those who never have to pay that is they do pay and then do fine or at least better than those who haven't got any money money I have to cover my tracks I don't know what fate has in store for me and at this point in my life I can't talk about fate my fate is probably already decided and I don't know if I've got to protect my last years with decency with the money I'll try to buy myself a nice little business one of those that never go broke that way I'll have some peace of mind I'll buy some kind of food business that people always need something like a bakery or a small grocery store I'll have to find out which takes less work or I'll buy a newstand and spend the whole day sitting and reading the newspaper and chatting with the neighbors no that's not my kind of business I need something to keep me lively undoubtedly what I've got to do is get out of circulation The Duke died he's dead I never knew him he was just an illusion a great moment and nothing more a few years of glory and then to live the memory among criminals con men traffickers all kinds of

The city at night.

The Duke enters the Cabaret Voodoo. He leans against the bar and orders a drink. Red lighting predominates. Also the glow from the glasses and the bottles. The dark pockets of the tables. The naked shoulders of the women of the night. Isolated laughter, generally in the corners. The four starving musicians listlessly playing their instruments. The women who have no escort are grouped together at a table gossiping without any drink, waiting for someone to make them an offer. A couple is doing a clumsy dance on the dance floor. The orchestra finishes and is about to begin The Duke's number, his set, his momentary obsession. The lisping dame makes the introduction and the drums drown her out. Nobody cares. The lights go down. Silence. In the dark you can make out the figure of a body that moves to the center of the stage. The music bursts forth, probably out of tune. A brilliant light falls on a body covered by a flowing cape. The hips move in gentle accompaniment to the rhythm. The dancer sways over to the piano, turns, and lets the cape drop. She is wearing a provocative dress slit up the sides. The Duke is wild about her breasts. They are the most aggressive ones he's ever seen. He sips his drink without taking his eyes off her. He knows she's the owner's woman but he can't hide his passion. There have even been times when he has provoked her deliberately. But the water never reaches the river. He drinks nonstop. She is a part of the music. She has already let her dress fall to the floor and all she is wearing now is that strange getup with the little balls that knock together and annoy him no end. The Duke already knows this dance by heart. He knows that when the drums go into their solo she will let her hair down, and that when the trumpet comes in again she will take the brassiere with the little balls off and then her two breasts will attack without compassion. He knows she will place her hands on the back of her neck and sweep her hair up so that her breasts stand out even more. More and more. The Duke knows this whole routine. He is a part of it. The waiters and the women also know it. Even she knows it. He always promises himself he won't come. For more than a month now he comes every other night to participate religiously in this spectacle. In dozens of other cabarets there are tons of dancers like her, better ones too. Yet every other night he walks down the stairs of that filthy basement, bearing the defiant humiliation she inflicts on him when, like now, she approaches the closest tables and then the bar, where she knows he is, shaking and twirling god knows how those two traitorous doves. She's stopped in front of him, smiling. He knows she puts her all into it in order to arouse him. She moves her hips slowly and sticks her pointy tongue out. The lisping old lady mutters from behind the bar, 'Thatta girl.'

She approves of the sensualness of the dancer's movements as she makes her provoking sounds, just like the round spot that illuminates the dancer and now spreads out to include him in its glare. The Duke takes a drink. And smiles. She returns to the center of the dace floor and ends her number lying on the floor, sweeping it with her hair. The music changes. He drinks. Two more and he will leave, slowly climbing the stairs and bearing on his shoulders the sarcastic looks of the ones who know what it's all about. He drinks and drinks. Now it's time to pay and leave. Another drink. He drinks and drinks. He jumps down from the stool. Decisive. He crosses the dance floor. He enters a corridor he's unfamiliar with. He hears voices. He goes towards them. A door. That's the voice. He opens the door. She is pleasantly surprised . . . The old dame with the lisp shrieks for him to leave. He shoves her out of the way and grabs the two traitorous doves. The old lady exits screaming. He avidly, desperately drinks them in. He is surprised to see that he is not repulsed. He squeezes, caresses, bites delicately, kisses the cheating doves. The owner stalks in. Just as his left thigh feels the warm dampness. The first shove catches him off guard and he falls to the floor. The old dame shouts and the beauty assumes the look of a woman taken advantage of. The Duke gets up and, although he's drunk, lands his blows with precision and ruins his rival's face. But others get in the act, the waiter and the bouncer. Now it's more difficult. But he still can handle them. He leaves the dressing room in order to have more room. They're tough and some of the blows get him. The old gal with the lisp runs out to phone. He catches her with the mouthpiece in her hand and lands a blow right to her hemorrhoids. Chairs and bottles are flying. Screams of whores and a general mass exodus. Finally, thanks to the exertion, he is no longer drunk but he can't stand up. He must see it through to the end. He hits and is hit. His reflexes are still fast. These makeshift opponents can tell that. Who knows, maybe they even paid once to see him fight in the ring. Drums and cymbals be damned. The Duke feels fine. He's right where he belongs. He knows this kind of language, it's his specialty, he's the boss here. There's a difference between hitting barefisted and with gloves on. Gloves can numb, stun, knock over. But fists land blows that really hurt, both the giver and the receiver. And when you're used to landing a knockout blow with the glove, you can't understand why the same blow without the glove doesn't have the same effect. The blow is the same but your opponent doesn't fall. It's hell to have to learn the same routine twice. But The Duke knows he has to and puts his whole soul into it. And he wins. The lights go on. The disaster is widespread. He can pay for it. The opponents rise and start to clean the mess up. Everybody and everything in its place. They sweep. The orchestra playing is the one that does the tangoes. The old dame comes in with the cops.

'That's him, that's the one!'

The owner says that there's no problem, nothing's happened, just a little party that got out of hand. The policeman feels uncomfortable. The tango singer bellows forth:

'Arrest me, sargent, and put me in chains.'

He ended up singing his tango at the station.

'A great guy, as far as I am concerned. The only dealings I had with him is when he came by to buy cigarettes. But he seemed like a nice person. Sometimes he wouldn't be in a hurry and would linger to talk, generally in the morning. My kid was a real fanatic, and when I told him that he often came by to buy cigarettes from my stand, he insisted on hanging around until he could see him. At first he was too shy even to say hello to him, but then he got so he would chat with him. He was an easy sort to talk to. I really don't have anything to say. I don't believe any of the stuff they say about him. He was always sensational with me. When my kid got sick he went to see him right away, I didn't even have to ask him twice. He even took him a present. A little train. He always told him to study hard and not to be a boxer. Strange, huh? Him saying that you shouldn't be a boxer . . . He often told me things about his life. He liked to talk to me because I would listen. He seemed to be sad that he couldn't help his mother. She died when he was in an orphanage. Perhaps luck didn't treat him any too well despite the fame he had. I like boxing, but real boxing, boxing with style and vigor. You can't fool me saying that boxing is the art of defense and nothing else. It's the art of defense and the intelligence of attack. The Duke was all that. My kid used to like just throwing punches and nothing more. I never could get him to see the real art of the sport, that is until we went to see The Duke. It was a great experience for him, and it really opened his eyes. The Duke was like a magnet, a real charmer who commanded respect. A lot of rivals said they were going to beat him and when the referee would be telling them the rules you could see their faces filled with fear. My kid always followed him, he even had an album. It was easy to get to know him because my stand is close to the stadium. But he was never really a client until after he stopped fighting, or after they made him stop fighting, because of that problem with his eye. He had bad luck. I'm convinced he could have gone on to be a world champion, mark my words. When he was fighting he took care of himself real good. A day wouldn't go by when he wasn't training, he only smoked a little, and he was real serious about his profession. My kid even followed him when he was in training. No, just listen to me. As long as he was fighting he smoked very little, I'd almost say he didn't smoke at all. Of course, afterward he smoked a lot, and he drank more than he should've. Tell you anything strange? The truth is I can't think of anything unusual to tell you . . . He liked to dress well. He was a little timid. When he lingered to talk he would sit on that stool and he would get over close toward the wall so that people wouldn't recognize him easily. No, my kid paid a lot of attention to him, and he didn't become a boxer. Well, really he's a grown boy, but I call him kid just out of habit. He's studying law and is a volunteer fireman. Yeh, when he told me he was going to become a volunteer fireman, I told him he was nuts, but then I realized I was the crazy one. He wasn't cut out to work the stand. It looks like an easy job, but it's a tiring one and it kind of turns you into a bum, I don't know if you get what I mean. Anyway, if he wanted to be a volunteer fireman that was his business, as long as he doesn't become a thief or a murderer he should be what he wants to, right? Don't mention it. Thank *you*.

stinking vermin the only thing of The Duke left to me is a broken nose and nothing else why bother to recall better moments when you're in worse ones it's like you wanted to punish yourself and that's not what I want I want to get out of this hole and save the last years of my life I could open a new dive with women but no no no no I've got to forget that sort of thing they never turned out well for me always a headache I've got to realize that I don't handle that sort of business well I always end up losing the best thing would be a small grocery store I'll try to get a decent and hardworking wife even one who's half moron as long as she's not a bitch and then to wait for death calm and peaceful in any case I still have a few years to live happily despite my lungs but if I enjoy the ten or fifteen years I have left too much I'll end up falling again and then maybe I won't be able to get up again and the chance I have right now is the only one I've got a nice fat wad of large bills doesn't come along every day maybe if I watched my drinking I could enjoy these few years without ruining things again what Mirna told me is a lie that I'm an alcoholic when I want to stop I can and I can easily go two days without drinking a drop besides no matter how much I have to drink I always know what I'm doing it was Flaco who got me started on wine of course it was because of the cold where can Flaco be these days people can lose track of each other just like that Flaco was a good guy when we came back a real mess from digging the trenches he still had enough strength to read by candle light those strange books about Indians Flaco knew about everything if you had seen him you wouldn't have given a plugged nickel for him yet he was true blue just like blood as the saying goes it rises to the wound without being called I remember I had some problem with Petiso one day I couldn't take it any longer and we got into a real knockdown dragout and along comes Flaco and puts an end to it he did his best for us all to live in peace he knew absolutely everything about Indians their history their struggle against the soldiers their forms of life how they had been killed off little by little until there were only a few tribes scattered here and there finally one day me and Petiso really got into it out in the middle of the desert and everyone sat down around us there slugging it out in the middle by that time we were all in great shape because of the work and the two of us were ready to go all the way I was lucky because I split his lip and his brow and there was a lot of blood so they stopped the fight with a partial victory for me truth is we were about equal and he hit really hard and I was wearing down if luck hadn't given me those two blows Petiso probably would have finished me off but that's the way life is like the time of the title fight everybody was convinced I'd win we argued with the German about my cut the son of a bitch shafted us royally making us pay for all the food and saying he'd never said it was on him same thing about the hotel we almost slugged it out but he threatened to call the police saying we were filthy communists it was the first time I'd heard that word in the bar we split the money since the guy had already paid for everything and everybody happy with the money in their pockets we started to plan the immediate future the majority wanted to go to the station and buy the tickets at first Lungo and someone else wanted to stay a month more I joined them because what we'd earned digging ditches despite the holdup was quite a bit of money a lot more than you could make in an honest job in the city during the three months we went to the cathouse and instead of boring the women we kept on about the benefits of staying another month under another contractor a more honest one or whether we should get out Flaco had already talked with other people and had gotten a better arrangement than the one the German offered who everybody knew to be the biggest bloodsucker around little by little the ones who wanted to go won out the ones who missed their girlfriends who wanted to see their parents and by the time we left the cathouse it had been decided we would return home at dinner Flaco says he's staying and will continue to explore the Indian territory you'd almost believe from the way he looked he was a native in reality he looked like an Englishman or a movie actor who played romantic parts the only problem was he was missing a front tooth and the rest were all decayed or yellow from smoking I decided to stick with him and visit other towns if I didn't do it then I would never do it that night we all slept in the station and the next day we said goodbye to our friends I hugged Petiso and advised him not to fight again until his scars had healed well otherwise they might open again in those days I had intuitions about scars that later I would hardly have the train left we went to a gas station and got them to give us a highway map for truckers we studied it carefully and decided to head west toward the mountain ranges it looks like it's getting cold my esteemed little rat don't you want a drink Flaco was the one who taught me how to drink he drank when it was cold and when it was hot I started out drinking only when it was cold and then just for the hell of it we decided to shave since we had an hour to kill before the bus left we did it in the bathroom of the station this place had served us great as a hotel without our ever bothering the employees of the place the first stop unless I'm wrong was called El Puma and was in a pretty high spot it wasn't much more than four humble huts there was nothing for us to do there we had already agreed that we would travel as free as possible we would buy tickets to a certain place but if along the way we liked a town well we would stay there with no further problem we had also agreed that if one of us stayed behind or went on ahead alone that was fine and no questions asked as the towns went by we swallowed many different colors of dirt and the people traveling with us were fewer and fewer in number I woke up one afternoon because I struck my head on the window and discovered that it was only us and the driver crazy about his motorized puppy despite the bumping around Flaco was still asleep with his head buried in his chest and his hands between his legs stretched out in front of him for a moment I felt a certain chill to be in the middle of such immensity evidently we were a long long way from the nearest town than we were when we were working on the ditches but when I realized that the only one responsible for me was me I calmed down the driver realized I was awake and shouted to me that in half an hour we would be arriving I was surprised to see a ñandú run by it seemed so unreal to me since we had never seen one except in the zoo that is to say I felt pleasantly surprised with this apparition it was worth the trouble to have made this trip just to see it run after a while there was another one and I woke Flaco up he was also fascinated by the animal's elegance as he ran they were gray and really very funny like you little ratty friend oh the tingling in my forehead is starting to hurt a drink would calm my nerves finally we got there and despite having slept during the ride we had to rest since the town was low we couldn't see much when we arrived so where the driver stayed we stayed too in a fairly large house with large patios that functioned as a hotel when some stranger from out of town happened by we later found out it was the only one in town we took a shower and got rid of the last flea on us when we got to the dining room to eat the owners looked at us with faces a lot friendlier than when we arrived we ate and slept in starched white sheets we could hardly believe it starched sheets not too much but just enough to guess that if that's how they did the sheets shirts would probably be stiff as steel to wake up in a town at the foot of the Andes is more than just a privilege it is to be illuminated by the sky when you are about to open your eyes you feel that the colors will be different from the ones you know even the air you breathe there is like being at peace to breathe well I mean enjoying the air that floods your lungs Flaco was shaving he shouted to me from the bathroom that we had to watch our appearance the first day until we could see what the possibilities of the town were we had one of those breakfasts you only hear about and while Flaco stayed chatting with the owners I went on out unable to resist it any longer and there before my eyes was the prettiest sight I had ever seen the Andes sweeping up from under my feet to the very top so imposing proud full of mystery provoking awe in me like a kid some of the slopes were red some green brown and white extending in folding curves I remember that at that instant I felt very happy I breathed in the air with gusto filling even my heels and I exhaled slowly like it was a friendly greeting to nature profoundly at peace with the world I started to walk through the town of low white houses with the warm sun playing on their sides the wide cobblestoned streets made me remember cowboy movies I really think now that it was all a dream moreover I remember that I was strutting like a peacock when a girl came around a corner and said hi to me I stopped short it was so unexpected when I got ahold of myself the girl had already gone way past me people not too many out walking and a very pretty girl had said hi to me I ran to the hotel to tell Flaco about it the jerk popped my bubble right off telling me that she had greeted me like she would say hello to anyone here that's the way they are besides everybody knows everybody else and they all greet each other and tourists are scarce here so they also say hello to them as though they were one of them this isn't the big city pal he said and here I thought I was going to make it with even the chickens so I had to make do with the spectacular scenery offered by the Cordillera it'll probably rain again it'll keep on intermittently until tomorrow and you're sleeping my dear ratty friend if I try to feed you from my hand you'll likely bite me right or wrong huh answer aha so you'll have to see what my intentions are and just what would you like my intentions to be except for purely honest ones what can I ask from you except your natural and disinterested friendship oh with all due respect you tell me that as far as you're concerned your friendship with me would be

On a stage decorated by weak lights and a worn curtain, a stripper executes her number with obvious boredom. The guy in charge of lighting, a dwarf in a torn shirt, seated in one of the boxes no longer used by anyone, works the faded revolving disk of the spot. The result is an irritating illumination that ends up making the few spectators scattered about the immense theater dizzy. Sorel, Walter and The Duke *occupy seats far away from each other.* Sorel *is busy scrutinizing the entrance of the spectators, who are guided by the usher. Despite all the rouge she has on the stripper is unsuccessful in hiding her leprous lip. A tall, heavy-set, bald man arrives. The thug who serves as usher mechanically shines his light along the floor and moves on ahead without waiting. When he reaches the second row he finds he's lost his passenger: the tall, heavy-set, bald man has taken a seat in the back rows where our three heroes are sitting. The usher moves in among the rows and demands his tip, which he has no trouble getting. Another stripper comes on, one with stringy varicose veins. The new arrival changes seats, once, twice. Over to the darkest side. He leaves his briefcase on the seat next to him.* Sorel, *like a shadow, slips over to the next row and places himself exactly behind the tall, heavy-set, bald man. In* Sorel's *hands you can see the glint in the blackness of the air of a fine, silvery thread. The one with the stringy varicose veins leaves the stage and a more respectable looking one comes on. The tall, heavy-set, bald man becomes enthralled. His right shoulder moves in time with the music. With singular dexterity* Sorel *lashes the silvery wire out with his right hand and grabs it with his left hand. The tall, heavy-set, bald man probably thinks it a vicious fly.* Sorel *joins the two ends together and pulls firmly, turning his hands as though working a tourniquet. The tall, heavy-set, bald man doesn't even have time for a final sigh, at best just a slight movement of his foot against the seat in front of him. On the way out,* Walter *gives the usher-thug a friendly pat on the back:*

'When the hell are you guys going to give us some new strippers, huh?'

self-interest aha well I can't say that you're dishonest and why might you be interested if I oh well since I would then take real good care of you and in exchange you'd give me ah whatever I'd want okay that's fine I'd like something very simple to die in peace and without realizing it what do you think about my request ratty rat huh then we're in agreement huh okay you want me to continue fine we spent barely two days in the town after seeing everything there was to see which wasn't much except for the beauty of the place fishing down at a creek and chatting with the owners of the hotel we realized we had to continue our trek because there wasn't even the chance of any decent date luck was with us the third day while we were finishing lunch a light plane landed in the middle of a field and the pilot brought out the majority of the townspeople it turned out he was an American and no one understood a thing no matter how hard the guy thought up the most ingenious gestures people in small towns are very pure and no matter how hard they tried they couldn't figure out what the new arrival wanted someone hazarded the guess that the two strangers who had arrived a couple of days ago might know English and they came over to our table I was quite surprised when Flaco said sure he knew English and stood up wiping his mouth with the napkin I would never have guessed that a bum like him who had spent ten years wandering around the country from one end to the other and who only read books about Indians could know anything about English so we sat down with the guy at a table we set up special with some steaming cups of coffee and I saw with surprise how Flaco mumbo-jumboed around I thought I caught some of it when they said redio I surmised they were probably talking about the radio and sure enough they were Flaco glanced up at the entire town crowding around the table because they all wanted to know what was going on and asked the owners if there was a superultrasonic radio in the town to make contact with the capital of course no one had that kind of radio at night they could barely pick up a few stations on their elementary sets Flaco kept on working at a conversation and I realized that he wasn't exactly anything fluent to judge by the worried and desolate face of the American finally we got up and set out toward the light plane a pretty little job all painted red a dream with the whole town at our heels no doubt that this would be a historic day for the whole area the guy had to get some kids down from the wings where they were hanging and we helped out as best we could until that moment I had no idea what was going on in Flaco's mind I saw them stick their heads in the plane and that the guy pointed out two forward seats and two smaller ones and Flaco tells me make it snappy with the suitcases he'll take us north I told him there's no one here who can fix his radio but that they would probably fix it in a town I knew about great I answered and what town is that I added he kept on running while saying I haven't the faintest notion I guess in some town we'll find along the way we've got to hurry before he takes off alone we put everything in my bag and his cardboard suitcase we paid the owner who because he was a good fellow gave us a discount and the next second we were clambering aboard the airplane with the whole town cheering us on like we were setting off to cross the south pole I took a seat in the back because I could see better without the interference of the wings the guy insisted I put the seat belt on I didn't want to after all I told myself what could possibly happen in that little machine and besides I could see better without the seat belt impeding my view we took off while my heart beat excitedly with the sensation of climbing up up up and seeing everything below getting littler and littler I was so excited about seeing the fields little patches of the prettiest colors I had failed to look out the other side Flaco who was traveling in front turned around and shook me and pointed out through the other window because of the noise we couldn't hear each other except by shouting when I saw the other view I almost wet my pants with the indescribable joy of so much beauty all in one place it was tremendous to see the Andes from high up but not from too high up just a few meters above them you can't imagine it because it gives you the sensation that you could reach out the window and grab a handful of snow and what to say about the light reflected off of the snow there were little hidden suns behind the rocks it was all the unending thrill of seeing with your own eyes one marvel after another one surprise after another like the way I banged my head on the roof of the plane the ones in front didn't notice what happened but I almost fainted luckily they were never able to count to ten with me and I recovered from the blow what happened was that we fell into air pockets flying around the Andes and in one of the pockets the small plane dropped suddenly without warning and I really paid for my stupidity in spite of the blow I continued to be thrilled about what I saw the plane continued cruising around the peaks I don't need to say that I finally put my seat belt on like I should have the blow on the head was enough to convince me we entered an area full of air pockets and we dropped and climbed like a roller coaster this movement started to give me problems with the meal I had just eaten and I tried to forget my air sickness otherwise I thought I would die moreover the Yankee who didn't like us to call him the Yankee he already told Flaco so let go of the wheel he put the automatic pilot on and started taking photographs from different angles when I say from different angles I don't mean he moved the camera around the nut moved the plane around and as a result we would suddenly find ourselves in the wildest positions I swear when we were on our side with the wings straight up and down I just about lost my lunch but I closed my eyes and thought about the first thing that came to my mind I breathed deeply and saved the situation the Yankee took the wheel again and we breathed easier the plane went in along the entire range of mountains we cruised over the highest peaks as though we were going to give them a hug we discovered rivers which seen from up high could only be called beautiful the Yankee took out a map and tried to locate the reality that matched the drawing he sometimes matched them up and he would enthusiastically motion to us that we were passing exactly over the place on the map he was pointing to little by little we felt more at ease with him and Flaco would indicate to him that we should go over that way and after a while he was acting like the commander and the Yankee paid attention to him because he was supposed to be telling him how to get to that town and since he had the map would he tell him where it was I observed how Flaco was in a jam but he quickly wriggled out of it pointing with his finger farther to the north I realized his idea was to get us as far away as possible and that's how it worked out we passed over various small towns that looked straight out of children's books we came to the end of the Andes and we could make out a rather large town the Yankee was happy to see it and he patted Flaco on the shoulder we made a perfect landing and climbed down from our delightful dream the Yankee was delighted to see people who could speak English and not garble it like Flaco and moreover who would fix the radio system of the plane he invited us to have something to eat with him and after such a whirlwind trip we were starved since we knew we wouldn't always be able to eat decently on our trip we took him up on the offer and ate everything on the menu after all the cost was peanuts to him but for us it was a holiday anyway he had to express his gratitude to us in some way we finished up with a cup of black coffee and foreign cigarettes a very fancy brand they came in cardboard boxes that Yankee must have been an eccentric millionaire and quite intelligent since he knew how to enjoy life he was probably traveling all over the world like that in the back seat he had all his clothes hanging up on wooden hangers all rather sloppy we said our goodbyes with effusive handshakes and my pal said good luck in English so he told me later we went out to roam around the town the climate was not quite as cold at least in the afternoon we quickly found our way around and checked into a small hotel almost on the outskirts next to a tiny station where a little train left regularly it looked like a toy as usual the owners were a married couple but not natives the front part served as a bar and it looked nice and quiet the room was small but comfortable and there were enough blankets in any case I always used the blanket I had been carrying around from the beginning we complained about the price a bit and got a discount we went out to walk around me still wearing my cap with earmuffs and a three-day beard Flaco shaved immediately he was always prepared for some fun right around the corner there was just one movie theater next to the single bar and both were owned by the mayor or the boss of the town all there was left to see were some modest houses scattered around the attractive and expensive houses concentrated in the center of the town and there were more on the outskirts residential spreads or mansions we later found out that they belonged to the wealthy landowners damn I wish I could live in a place like these Flaco murmured that night when we returned to our room to go to bed we discovered a group of men in the bar *meaner looking than death and dirty drunk some of them were dancing together overlooking good manners we had the same opinion about a lot of things and as far as problems were concerned we were in agreement that we had to avoid them at all costs we took the long way around and went in the back way when we were in bed my friend surprised me by saying he liked the owner's wife I muttered something between my teeth and covered my head damn it I said I had seen her first I was charmed by the cut of her face her wide jaw I really liked that in a woman besides there was a certain mystery about her and she was a lot younger than her husband he looked a little lonely and was in there getting drunk to the gills with the rest of the fellows that marriage had problems next day we got up and she had our breakfast ready a nice full one we had made arrangements to pay her a breakfast like that would last us all day without eating we exchanged a few words but she had good control over herself when Flaco tried to find a friendly opening she saw it coming and went off to the kitchen we went out for a walk it was already about eleven o'clock in the morning and let me tell you walking around that town was just like being in heaven I can't think of anything better of course we had the Andes right close by not as close as in the last town but close enough to still enjoy them because it was just like a woman nature*

'What can I tell you? He was a killer. Huh? So now that he's dead we're supposed to say he was a great guy? He was a killer, a provocateur. What can you expect from guys like that? Did they ever work in their lives? What would you like to drink? Hey, Carlitos, a vermouth for the gentleman here! They go in for boxing because they don't like to work and they're bums from the time they're born. On the other hand guys like us bust our buns all our lives, here behind the counter. You've got to be on this side. Don't think it's easy, just a matter of coming in, opening the cash register, and filling your pockets with cash. No, you've got to always be here, checking up on the help. If you turn your back they'll even steal your socks, don't think they won't. Don't make me laugh. Well, what can I tell you, I never liked the guy. He came in almost every morning, let's say every other day. Sometimes a week would go by without seeing him. He would start playing by himself, like a dog. Yeh, he was kind of good with the cue, that's the truth. But, don't you see, pool and boxing, pastimes for bums . . . Come on, don't tell me. While he was messing around the pool table, there were others working to make something of this country. Sure, I'm part of the workers. Look here, you can't tell me that games like that help the country out. Let's be serious. He was a troublemaker. Once two boys were watching him play and he almost split their heads open with the cue. Believe me, he was a nut. I know what I'm talking about. Boy, I sure never bothered with him! What can you expect? If he comes in and pays his bill, I'm not going to throw him out. Besides he would come in the morning and at that time of day there would be nobody playing . . . That's what I'm trying to tell you, while decent people were making a living he was in here playing. Your problem is you don't want to see my point. They all end up the same way . . . Sure, sure. Hold on, okay, you're right there. They don't all end up bad, but the ones who go straight are the exception to the rule, my friend, don't you see? The ones who end up ok are careful and no one is looking over their shoulder at them like they were with The Duke. Duke! Hell, he had a lot of nerve calling himself The Duke. A guttersnipe who probably didn't have a mother. That's always the way it is, believe me, it's hard for a guy not to get mad. All of our idols are scum, that's not hard to see . . . I know the night . . . No, my partner and I take turns. Of course. Like I said, I know the night. I know how idols are made. We Argentines don't like people who'll bust their butts working, only the ones with shady, hard-luck stories, the ones who are failures and end up busted. They're the ones we turn into idols! Of course, my friend. We like to admire failure in others, their downfall . . . Are you crazy! Sorry, I didn't mean to offend you, but you're nuts. Let's talk serious . . . Okay, but let me talk too. If you do all the talking, it's no fun. Hey, Carlitos, get the table behind the column. If we take turns talking, you'll see how we'll end up seeing eye to eye . . . Sure, of course. Now, just listen to me. We deserve what we have, right? It's like Lombroso said, each country has the sort of crime it deserves. What? Do you think just because someone works behind a counter he doesn't read? Come on, now! Look, let's try a little test, you name all the people you consider idols and I'll show you they're all scum, failures, and that they are idols because we enjoy other people's failure, and I'm including myself in the we. You'll see I'm not joking . . . Sure, even if it seems hard to believe, envy is our national patrimony. I know what I'm talking about, I know the world, I've been in a lot of different countries, don't think I was born behind this counter. There are places where the idols are decent people . . . See, didn't I tell you? You just named someone who isn't an idol, pal. No, he's nobody's idol . . . Yeh, I know he's got a company and makes money hand over fist. He's famous. But, damn it, he's no idol! . . . And I don't have to tell you his life story! He died from tuberculosis before his thirtieth birthday. Cheap women ran circles around him, and in his last fight it made you cry to see him kiss the mat. And everybody thrilled to death, and do you know why? Because we like to look down on people! But when the idol slips away from us and, instead of throwing his money away in cabarets, he saves it or invests it and makes good deals and such, we no longer like him as much, we think he's thumbed his nose at us. Pardon me, I don't want to be offensive, pal. But it makes my blood boil to see such hypocrisy . . . There's another one, yeh him. We agree on that, but just think about it a little bit, he's no idol, yep, even though he's been champ a thousand times or whatever, he isn't an idol! He's stopped fighting, has good health, takes care of himself and they may clap for him if they see him at a match, but he's not an idol. Make no mistake about it, the idols are the ones who are failures, because envy is our mother and grudge our father . . . Sure, that one was a fine musician, but later he always had his head in the clouds and everybody was happy because he was on the skids and they were there, happy to feel sorry for some poor dumb jerk . . . Come off it, my friend! Carlitos, get the check for that table over there. No, that guy was never any idol. He owned land, was a rancher and when he died no one even noticed. On the other hand, they would dress Tiger — you remember him, don't you — up to look like Chaplin, with a sign on his back advertising children's shoes. And he was an idol, pal! . . . Now, that one's not an idol either. He's intelligent, he's gotten into movies lately, he's no dope. And you know damn well that no one goes out to the airport to greet him. He's got my admiration. He'll die a ripe old age in a soft bed. He won't satisfy all the ones that would like to see him die busted. He sure is bright . . . Now, that one, poor fellow, he's an idol all right. Hasn't even got a rusty old blade to shave with and now he's working somewhere as a doorman. Look let me tell you something. A few days ago a friend of mine came by and started to tell me about The Duke as a fighter. I don't deny he was a fighter, and he was telling me about what a boxer Ramírez was. Ah, he was a real boxer, and the last time I saw him he was running an elevator. You get my point? He said he was better off because he had seen him running an elevator. Because he was worse off than my friend. You think what I'm saying doesn't make any sense? Look, why don't we talk about lost oxen and be done with it . . . No, buddy, I'm not getting mad, but if you're swimming in shit you want everybody to jump in with you . . . Yeh, sure. When will you run the photo . . . ? No, I was just asking because I change shifts tomorrow.'

wearing a pink wrapper whispering a submissive goodnight of course I answered her friendly as though saying I was sorry for the interruption I supposed that Flaco was going to land on me for bothering them but no so he was happy I had finally gotten back because he hadn't been able to get rid of her she had become a bore and was talking about love I quickly got into bed trying to be careful so he wouldn't notice my trembling face we spent about a month that way he busy with the owner's wife and I playing pool in the bar of the movie with the local hotshots they all had late model cars and even though they only lived four blocks away they would go to the bar in the car almost nobody ever walked the streets of that town the only ones who would be on the street were the sheep and lambs one day I played a round with the mayor and won they weren't very nice about it I realized the mayor had suddenly become very tense with his loss and so I had to allow him to win the next round I couldn't allow him to have a grudge and maybe kick us out of town or something worse he won two rounds off me and I said that I must have won the first game by sheer luck he was pleased and invited us all to have a drink and we swilled like pigs one glass after another someone dropped the comment your friend sure knows how to have a better time right I was startled and in a flash I saw a series of images in which the hotel owner walked into our room with a huge knife and gushes of blood bathed the walls I got myself under control and very serious said unfortunately my friend is in bad health and can't stay up till all hours of the night besides he prefers to read history books on the other hand I like pool and I laughed like a regular imbecile the mayor grasped the situation and turned it in my favor I was really smart to lose against him as a consequence I could count on him in any future jam about that time our money started to run out not because we had paid the hotel bill since the owner's wife didn't charge us a thing although she would give us a receipt just in case but because we had been careless with our drinking especially ordering beer in the bar and my expenses at the whorehouse so I tried to scare Flaco a little and he was getting tired of the woman's hints about the two of them running away together he paid attention to what I was saying about rumors in the town and that it would be better for us to change hotels or just to get out of town since we no longer had any business to tend to in the town we strolled around on the outskirts and found a modest place where drinks and food were sold to the poor to the

Indians to the farm workers and to the few individuals working on a two-story construction project at that time that was considered a skyscraper in the town two acceptable girls took the orders they weren't beauties but you could talk to them of course by that time we already had somewhat of a reputation in the place since neither of us sucked his thumb I in the whorehouse and he at home sick but my friendship with the mayor who besides wanting to teach me chess surrounded us with kindness of course we were in like Flynn so it was a matter of packing up our bags and cashing in our warm bed the hotel owner gave us a fond farewell poor guy I wanted to make a wide circle around the town so no one would see us but Flaco wanted to take the direct route right through town as though it didn't matter in any case there was no one around it was about noon and the first car came by at about two in the afternoon we took up our places without considering the consequences Flaco began to sell his sandwiches and beer as though he'd done it all his life from the first night I had a premonition dear ratty rat you can understand would you like a drink you can understand how dumb we were instead of getting out of there after having left the woman behind oh how stupid you'll never do anything like that when you make tracks make tracks for good get lost disappear go underground as deep as you can and wait for time which heals all wounds to do its thing and cover all of the woes of men with a veil yes ratty rat the drama was terrible the owner's wife a woman in the end considered herself to have been poorly treated worse used and humiliated and the poor thing was right since Flaco showed up at the movies with the other woman it seems that the deceived husband had had to spend a dark black night like hell itself with the woman flinging in his face how little a man he was in bed that she was no dope and for as long as Flaco had been in the hotel she had enjoyed him every night because he was a man a real man in bed and the husband struck by a bolt of lightning in his drunken stupor showed up in the middle of a dog's night that the rain had foreseen in its sense of drama he crashed into our room like a hurricane and stabbed the knife into Flaco's chest caught completely off guard he didn't even have time to set his mate *down on the table I could feel the blade penetrating my own body that dead head falling down on the table and that arm hanging down on one side could have been my own the screams of the women brought me back to reality the husband held Flaco against the chair and withdrew his knife* during that short interval I noticed that he was all disoriented he was just getting around to realizing that he had taken a man's life fright filled his face and he began to cry while the women kept on screaming like madmen and the thin one slapped my friend's face trying to make him wake up from his unreal dream the husband ran out I did too not to catch him but to go to the mayor's house I knew that at that hour he would have already left the bar while I was knocking on his door with the brass knocker I could see ending my days in a cell or hanging from the gallows my fright was so strong but everything in life works out my dear ratty rat it's just that at times one is simple minded and drowns in a glass of water first off the mayor gave me a big glass of whiskey that calmed me down somewhat and then we went over to the police chief's house and then to the scene of the crime the women had put him on the bed on top of some rags so the blood wouldn't make a mess of everything I noticed that the two men were a bit annoyed over the problems the whole business would bring to the town up till then they could consider clean as far as murder went they deliberated a long time in a corner and then called me over and explained to me that it was necessary to move fast since this matter should not get out so as not to sully the image of the town at a time when they were receiving large loans for public works and to stimulate tourist trade not a bit of it so we carried the body under the driving rain to a faraway place where the injured husband who the police chief had gone to get dug a deep grave where my friend was laid to rest forever the two women and us three men said a few prayers while the rain ran down my whole aching body on the way back I listened to the words telling me to be intelligent and discreet under the circumstances without having slept I waited in the small station for the hour of the little toy train's departure I got on and made myself comfortable in the double seat where barely one would fit there was a seat for one by the other window a child could barely have sat in it I left completely alone accompanied only by the engineer whom I hadn't seen before I was asleep by the time we were out of the town it must be the wine makes my head hurt so much I don't think so wine calms me down so that's not it ratty friend how many are there in your family huh ah quite a lot huh and of course you guys rule the world you're everywhere when we least expect it you're going to eat us alive although I personally think there's a solution and that's to tame you right why not if you *all agree it's really to your advantage since you already live in the houses the only thing to be worked out would be certain conditions like meal time the same as we have to do with dogs and cats of course we would teach the cats not to chase you and then we would all live happily every day after what do you think about my suggestion you guys could wake us up in the morning just like dogs do licking the master's face is there really any difference right none at all you would have to get shots of course there's got to be some control right and instead of living in corners you would move about happy and free through all the rooms making the children happy in their mischievousness they would carry you around in their pockets to have a little fun when the teacher was wrapped up in a boring lesson what do you say I can make all the arrangements I know a lot of dames won't accept the idea and would prefer to continue living in the dumps but we can't be bothered with that either as far as you are concerned or as far as we are concerned at least we could try it right of course I can make you a promise about it I'm not The Duke for nothing right you're still in your prime Don José would tell me and he was right the bad thing was I would smoke and drink if I had taken care of myself I would still be champ no I never was but I was the best everybody would say it the champ without a crown and the champ with a crown broke his head against the wall what do you say about that ratty rat friend huh yep before all that working in one factory after another one factory after another one factory after another bouncing around like a football the same way from one rooming house to another my best memory is of the underwear factory but let me tell you first about the soap factory you have no idea what that was like my first job right off was to wrap the soap for washing clothes everything was so old so old some*

The Duke enters the stadium accompanied by the dancer from the Voodoo. As soon as the bleachers spot him they break into applause and cheers. The dancer, radiant in her hairdo, squeezes The Duke's arm, pleased with herself. The Duke, visibly moved, answers the crowd by raising his fist in the air. They take their seats at ringside. The crowd continues its fevered chant:

'Long live The Duke!'

'Champion of champions!'

'Duke, Duke, Duke!'

Just like in his best days. When he was the one climbing into the ring. A lot of people come up to say hello. Some of them very famous. Others less so. The majority, nobodies. The fans, after all. He lights the flashy dancer's cigarette. He decides not to smoke. He knows that if he breaks down and smokes a cigarette, someone will make a big issue out of it. Better to maintain his image in public. That's what his promoter taught him.

The prelim match is over. As things go, a real bummer . . . The dancer never stopped shouting during the matches, not even for the warm-ups. Time for the main fight to begin. When the contestants enter the ring, each has a big smile from his corner for The Duke.

The fight begins. By just seeing how they move, The Duke is ready to go. Clumsy movements, a lack of intelligence in the use of the left. He should have been a trainer. It's getting more and more difficult to find stylists. He had been lucky to find Don José. What has become of him? Poor fellow, when he found out about his recent job, he stopped coming to see him. He never saw him again. Not even in the neighborhood club. He's probably off in the provinces. A friend had reproached him for giving up being a trainer and, carrying his body loosely, he replied:

'I gave the country the best boxer in history, and that's saying quite a lot. If anyone comes along with someone better than The Duke, maybe I'll go back to training. But be assured that won't happen.'

Real bores, these boxers, no legs, no waist. The Duke remembers his fight against Potro Villafañe. That was his real triumph. No one believed he could beat him. Don José claimed the promoter wanted to ruin him and that he was rushing into the match. Potro had a real advantage as far as experience in the ring, a lot of power and confidence. Maybe that's what made him lose. There was something funny about that fight, and they never found out what it was. The promoter didn't show his face for a week. The Duke noted something cold in his greeting. Maybe he wanted him to lose? He never really made an effort to find out, and even less so now he was retired. Potro got the best press coverage. The Duke barely had one notice in a newspaper, and neither the note or the newspaper was really of any consequence. Don José was against accepting the challenge, but he was enthusiastic. Since Don José didn't want to leave him in the lurch, he trained him, on his word of honor, like no other boxer in the world had ever been trained. In two months he moved from the six points that Don José had given him to nine, which Don José had also given him. Don José was always there, taking care of him like a son, down to the last detail. And in the end . . . Potro never in his wildest dreams thought that this boxer, who recently had won some popularity and a nice nickname, would fight like his life depended on it. As far as he was concerned it was just one more fight. But for The Duke it was the most important thing since his birth. During the first round, studying him, Potro noticed that he couldn't get in close. No matter, he would trap him against the ropes. But in the second round he couldn't corner him, even though he had tried to do it in a neutral corner. He was used to nobody ever getting away from him. His footwork was fatal and they dropped like flies at the slightest sound of his glancing hooks. He was used to seeing how his opponents would close their eyes when he decided to attack like a crazy man. By contrast, The Duke had his eyes wide open and was looking at him calmly. He would have to wrap things up without messing around anymore. What bothered him most was The Duke's agility. He always looked taller, and they were supposed to be the same height. His gloves covered all his targets. Never mind, he'd wear the resistance of his guard down and when he lowers his gloves . . . It was the fifth round and The Duke's arms were still up there, his legs too and . . . And the crowd . . . It was terrible to hear his opponent's nickname from the bleachers, everybody's throat crazed by the excitement. And that stringbean not paying any attention at all, just there working out his plan of attack. Potro understood full well that The Duke had a plan. That's how he lost, when he thought about his rival's plan. He had never paid any attention to his rivals' plans of attack — they were the ones who had to worry about his, he was the killer. For the first time in his life he was faced by an unknown quantity. For the first time he had to think about someone else. He was sweating on the inside. To think about the other guy meant being on the defensive. To have the disadvantage. And The Duke's blows were getting home, they were worrying and bothering him. He let them get on his nerves. He struck out against a body and the body was thin air. Yeh! shouted the bleachers. In a clinch he felt a short jab to the liver and stumbled. He was stumbling? In the past it was always the others who stumbled. Their sweat and their breath mingled together. The Duke was breathing easy, but he wasn't. He insulted him. The Duke didn't even notice. He continued to dodge Potro's attacks, keeping his left in front of his face. Blocking his vision, tricking him like a child. He went after him against the ropes and found himself flailing the air. He swung around and got a tremendous blow from that left. They came from the most unbelievable directions: from above, from below. What should he do? In the seventh round the worst happened: The Duke had cut him on the eyebrow. He tried to fight the way he best knew how and to land decisive blows. He would have to put his whole soul into it. He would win by his superior power, he wasn't called Potro, colt, for nothing. That decision was fatal. The Duke responded with the same power or more. Brutally. Without pity. All of his blows had a single objective: Potro's head. He could feel them. He was aware that all the blows he had ever received in his fights were coming together now. His pride in exposing his face so others would hit it and get the surprise of their lives seeing him still smiling had been a stupid idea. Now he was getting a thousand blows for every one The Duke was actually landing. In a split second he felt he was losing consciousness. He stumbled, seriously. The referee had to work to separate them. How many rounds still to go? He had lost count. Only his heart, his pride, kept him standing. He wanted to give in, to throw in the towel once and for all. But he had to go on. Just like his rivals had, as long as they could. Perhaps . . . A lucky blow. A saving blow. But the blood from his eyebrow blinded him. He stumbled. In a fog he saw the spectators at ringside on their feet and shouting. With their arms in the air. With their fists in the air. He knew, intuitively, that those fists would strike him without mercy if they could. He never thought this could happen to him. He thought it would be just another fight. The world championship. But Potro was not about to give them the pleasure of falling, he wasn't going to be their sacrificial lamb. Traitors! He had one last motion of defense which The Duke handled well. Then The Duke set about striking him implacably on the head and the body. But mostly on the head. With those fists that felt like bricks. He was really holding up like a colt. There was a lot of stamina, will, and self-respect. He should have been down by now. Now just to hit harder. With all his might. Now that he's letting his guard down. He stumbles. He can't catch his breath. I can strike at his kidneys and his head. It looks like a KO. I've got to get him down with one clean blow. If he loses his balance, he'll go down on his own. He's tough. I've got to be tougher. In the kidneys. One the head. He felt it. It's all over now. But he won't go down, damn him . . . I've got to get him with hooks. That's it, right. I'm sure he must have felt that one down to his toes. It's like hitting a hollow wall. A hollow sound. His arms are hanging loose. Now. With all your might. He's falling, he's falling, he's falling! I swear you're going to fall.

Finally he fell. The crowd had not been mistaken. The confidence they had had in that promise had paid off with interest. From that night on the newspapers always wrote The Duke out in capital letters. Potro died two months later without ever regaining consciousness.

comrades they said these buildings and these machines dated from the time of Columbus everything was dark black little light walls dirty with black grease in a few places there were political slogans the owners of the factory ignored olympically by the second week they transferred me to the waxworks where the candles are made to be lit to the virgins or to be used when you can't afford to pay the light bill that was the hardest job I've ever had in my life perhaps even worse than when I was a child and worked as a construction apprentice they made me carry the baskets of sand up the ladder and by the third trip I would feel like my legs were sinking into my body I'll never do anything but curse those days it was before the meatpacking plant poor cows how they would treat them they would pass by on hooks while my fellow workers would perform their tasks some were still not completely dead when they would cut their legs off or peel the skin from their head the tub of unborn calves in the center surprises found in the stomachs of the cows perhaps that was why they would weigh more perhaps that was why they fought dying they knew they were defending another life the tub of unborn calves once some newspapermen dropped by and they were escorted all around the place except over where the tub was they wouldn't let them take our pictures either sitting around on the floor eating grouped around in corners like we were ratty rat dear friend I promise you I'm leaving this place for good today I swear it as The Duke you haven't any idea how I admire you you are invincible on the other hand the sheep hah would you like me to tell you how they would kill them first you hang them by a back leg like the cows and they go marching by Indian file one hand holds their head and the other slits them from ear to ear and *they go right on by now dripping blood still bleating bah bah bah and still moaning until they run out of blood and firm hands grab a hold of them with electric saws the cows are slit from top to bottom so there are now two steers you know something dear ratty rat friend I left the place because I never could get used to the blood but it wasn't the blood that bothered me not the blood because when I fought there also would be blood but that was between two men two equals instead there would be the still not dead beasts being sawed up would you like a sip of my wine it's good it calms my headache besides my mother had already died so why continue there Don José said to me you're still in your prime and I paid attention to him those were the only decent years of my life despite everything I was fascinated by what they had told me about the Jews they do the job differently I mean killing the animals some said it was worse and some said it was better because the animal suffers less and dies immediately they would work in a patio off to the side very early in the morning when we were punching in they would be leaving they would never allow us to watch I got there very early but they had already performed the religious ceremony and were preparing the cleaver it was a special cleaver very short so sharp that from where I was up above the blinding reflection of the edge could be caught I believe it was long and slender they wore long white coveralls white hats and the classic beards that came down to their chests they would kill only a few animals they also would catch a back leg with a chain but only to subdue the living animal's movement before we would haul them up we had already hit them with the sledge hammer they would hang them up still alive and with the head almost touching the ground sometimes the animals were difficult and would not allow themselves to be subdued and they would have to chase them around the patio and only with difficulty be able to chain them from over in one of the corners they would pull on the chain strung over a pulley and the cow while being pulled up would swing his body in the other direction from the pull of the chain and would bang his head against the white tiles of the wall now I understood why so many of the tiles were broken on the lower part of the wall they would haul him up and the animal would swing mooing moo moo moo moo moo evidently as a sign of protest and the fact that he didn't like the business at all they would right away grab him by the horns to stop his swinging and they would loosen up on the chain just enough so his head would touch the floor in the position in which he would be any attempt at defense would be useless hanging from a back leg and the front ones held by apprentices future professionals the one holding him by the horns would maneuver in such a way that the animal had no choice but to hold its head back and innocently offer his naked neck when he stopped kicking and thought the game was all over the guy with the knife would bend over and with stunning skill would open with a single slit the entire neck of the beast even cutting his esophagus from which a thick and steamy vapor would be emanating the moaning the mooing the ferocious cry would cease and there would be left in its place a weak and barely audible sound like the sound made by blood dripping down on the skin from the neck the head and the body would still be joined together by a slender thread but both now irremediably dead sometimes there would be one without horns and in that case to grab ahold of them the man would place the four fingers of his hands on the back of the head burying his thumbs in the cow's eyes that way his hands would be nice and steady and he could control the movements of the animal and neutralize them so that the brief operation could be carried out with dispatch and the community would be able to eat like its religion specified of course it's clear my interest in seeing this was because I wanted to know if the poor cow suffered less I could no longer stand to miss a blow every time I would get splattered by the gelatinous eyes I was the one crying out on the inside that's why I hustled my way into the waxworks it wouldn't have been half bad if the molds hadn't been so heavy the place was a real slimy pigsty I would fill the buckets with boiling wax at first I thought if a drop were to get on my hands it would shrivel my skin then I realized that the first impression is what scares you and after that it's all child's play since the wax dries and sticks to your skin and thus forms a layer like a glove I can't recall how many buckets were necessary to fill a mold while one is drying you're getting the next one ready you fit in the wicks which drop down from holes in the ceiling sometimes they would get cut off or run out and you would have to climb up and put a new roll on and drop the beginning of the wicking down and the mold would fill up with wax while the other one was already dry with a long blade about a meter long and sharp as a razor the wicks were sliced of with a clean blow and here's where there was a problem with having only two arms with a single heave you would have to lift the mold of thick metal holding the candles and carry it over to the table about one or two meters away I swear it to you ratty rat no more or less but for me it seemed like kilometers since the mold was so damn heavy that every time I had to lift it I prayed to the Virgin but all the same the effort made it seem like my heart was bursting from my rear believe me ratty rat I'm not lying you have the word of The Duke once I was able to set the iron mold down on the table really it was more a question of dropping it or throwing it than setting it down you took the candles out but since as I have already told you I more like threw the mold down and since the candles came out from the ends usually instead of coming happily into the world they would split so what do you say to that huh ah you don't get it well let me explain it to you better the mold had long holes on the bottom perpendicular through which the thread of the cotton wick would pass you fill these holes with liquid wax which as it dries forms the candle now they've got to be taken out I believe you had to separate the mold in two one part would come up and the other would still be holding the candles which as well as being seen from the top could be seen sticking out the ends so when I would throw the mold down on the table if I wasn't careful to keep the candles from popping out the bottoms would crack and as a consequence my production was minimal and when the others were done with their work with a minimum number of molds I always had to do an extra round well so you didn't really get it but don't worry about it I don't get it either why I barely remember the first job I had I told you about it didn't I are you sure you don't want a slug so okay you don't know what you're missing the elephant told the ant but I know what I'm getting the latter replied come on laugh a little my dear friend a few drops of rain are falling the rain has gotten tired of crying everybody is worn out life itself has a limit we should all die at the same time and then only nature would be left and nobody would get hurt huh what do you think what louder I can't hear you ah so violence is our natural inheritance huh that's why I think everybody should die at the same time that's the only way to save your life I would try to lift the mold heave it up on my shoulder but I would sway to the side and when I tried to lift with one heave it was death itself I ask myself was this job invented by supermen it was a laugh to see me among the other six all giants in that section they told me that all the new workers got that job to soften them up and that later they would be trans-*

ferred to soaps but some had gotten used to the job and preferred to stay in that section the time the mold slipped from my hands and fell to the floor it almost broke my leg you can all go to hell I said and stick the molds you know where they went two months without paying me they told me I couldn't leave the job and I would answer right back hah and let me tell you how do you remember it was the same deal with the Englishman finally they slapped me with some deduction and then they paid me you're still at the right age Don José would tell me what a great guy that Don José was I was lucky with him he helped me out in general I can't complain because a lot of people when I'm far away from here I'm going to sit down quietly and make a list of all of them and send them all an anonymous letter thanking them for having helped everyone else because if someone helps you he doesn't help just you but he also helps others and the one who was helped in turns helps someone else so what do you have to say ratty rat louder I can't hear you oh who did I help let me think about it I think I helped a lot of people let's see let's see Mirna I helped her she was the one who wanted to work in the dive I didn't ask her to it was her idea then I got used to the idea what fault is it of mine let us suppose that you bring breakfast to me in bed without my having asked you to that's your business right that's the way life is ratty rat friend are you sure you don't want a drink take it while you can because it's almost gone Don José caught me on the way out of the bottling plant I was waiting for the bus I had a two hour bus ride can you believe that I had a two hour trip each way of course why do you think I'm dropping out tonight and you are all going to remember The Duke everyone of you I promise you tomorrow by this time I'll be

From his auto Sorel *stands watch over the people entering and leaving a building. When he sees two men come out, he goes in. He goes up in the elevator. He is received by an old man and a boy. The office is almost empty. There is nothing but a table and two chairs and a telephone. They converse animatedly about the big demand for dollars and assure him that the business is going splendidly.* Sorel *inquires about what kind of dollars they are using. The good kind. The counterfeit ones have just been sold. They have all the earnings for the week.* Sorel *draws his pistol, leaving the two dealers stunned.*

'My apologies.'
'You're the one who's going to be sorry later.'
'No one will know.'
'Are you crazy? Do you intend to kill us?'
'Yes.'
'Don't be a fool.'

Sorel *smiles and pulls the trigger.*
He arrives at the airport. In the baggage section of the International Hotel he leaves the briefcase containing the dollars. He returns to the city. He drives very fast. He enters the office cautiously. Everything is just as he left it: the bodies are motionless. He calls on the telephone.

'Don Jorge?'
'. . .'
'Bad news. I'm at the office . . .'
'. . .'

'They've been killed. I just got here.'

'. . .'

'There's no doubt it was them. Fine. I'll look for them.'

Sorel crashes into an apartment unannounced. The two men he saw coming out of the building are together in bed. Before they can reach the weapons on the nightstand, he opens fire on them. He opens the wardrobe and throws everything out on the floor. He makes as much mess as possible without searching for anything. He leaves.

He enters a sumptuous building. He tries to keep the elevator operator from seeing his face by covering it with a newspaper he's reading. Before they answer the door, they make him wait. He goes in. There are a lot of women sitting around, drinking, conversing, reading. All in filmy attire. In some of the other rooms women and men are drinking together. Couples go into separate rooms. They take him into a sitting room. An older woman receives him. They are alone.

'What a pleasure to see you, Sorel! To what do I owe the honor of your visit?'

'I am sorry, but I have to kill you.'

'What!?'

'I should imagine you weren't planning to live forever . . .'

He fires the gun with a silencer. He goes out and shuts the door. He addresses the woman who accompanied him.

'I'll be right back . . . Ah, the lady wants them to bring her a nice hot cup of tea in half an hour.'

He calls from a public telephone.

'Don Jorge?'

'. . .'

'All negative, including the German woman.'

'. . .'

(Turning pale.) 'No . . . I went by later, just a minute before calling you.'

He hangs up the phone and stands there lost in thought. He walks away slowly. He stops. He runs over to his car and speeds off. He ignores the stoplights. He reaches his apartment. The door is unlocked. Inside there is complete chaos. All of his family massacred. He sits down and contemplates the bodies. Their pictures are sitting framed on one of the pieces of furniture. There is a picture of his church wedding. From a secret drawer he takes out papers and documents, his and his wife's passports and a bunch of bills. He stuffs it all into one of his pockets. He puts each body in its corresponding bed and draws the covers up over them. As he leaves he makes sure the door is good and locked.

faraway let them turn the hounds loose on me if they want and Don Jorge and Mocho can go to hell I have the right to live two hours going and two hours coming I slept in the bus that crossed the avenue the third I took two hours trip in three buses the first from the plant to the diagonal the second to the double avenue and the third crossing the main avenue into the province the drivers all knew me because I was always falling asleep and would be the only one left on the bus when we got to the end of the line and I would have to wait for the next bus out whenever but only if I hadn't fallen asleep again I would reach my destination after a long ride the drivers would wake me up before I could miss my stop drowsiness is terrible there's no way to overcome it right ratty rat friend I see you are all nice and asleep quietly asleep ah well you can tell you're with a friend stay calm sleep well if a cat comes along I'll make a stew out of him they called us swallow workers because they would only give us work during the season that is in the summer when people drink more soft drinks first off they would make us sign a paper in which we resigned from the job believe me ratty rat friend before he would give us the job we had to resign from it it was really wild the first day they would give you the white work clothes with the name of the soft drink on the breast pocket they wouldn't give you the clothes when you signed on because not everybody would come back the next day believe me it's true tossing crates around is no joke you've got to have done it before you can talk about it I got used to it then in the third season they asked me if I wanted to stay on and I told them I would love to but I was very sorry I had been sent a contract from Hollywood and I was looking forward to practicing my English the little shrimp got red with rage there was this country guy who started working when I did they were almost all from the provinces the swallow workers come from north south west and work like dogs during the summer months even Saturdays and Sundays and holidays and Christmas and New Years and Three Kings all of them for twelve or fourteen hours a day and then they go back home with their pockets full of money to get by during the rest of the year until the next season when they will be back offering to take on the most menial jobs they ask for their addresses and then send them a telegram imagine getting a telegram out in the middle of the corn fields from the soft drink company you can imagine how proud it makes their family feel they proudly say in two more seasons they're going to make him sales manager as I was saying there was this enormous giant who started working when I did he worked for half an hour and left without warning before he left he said I came here to work not to be treated like a prisoner I liked him because he dared to say out loud what everybody thinks from the first minute he starts working there but what they won't say because they need the money or there is no other job available hah my first day working in the factory hah as soon as I left I said I would never go back there but Mirna convinced me hang on just a while one of these days you've got to catch on and then you can handle it and it was true it was a matter of catching on in any case as soon as I would get home I would stretch out on the bed and she would pour liniment on my neck my shoulders my waist my hips my legs and my arms and rub like hell sometimes I would fall asleep in that position and she would cover me and then feed me when I got up to go back to the factory I swear they didn't chase us with whips like you might suppose ratty rat friend it was just a question of being there to see it you would get in line alongside the whole length of the moving belt that comes up from below and goes on up above and you usually work with your companion there is another pair in the same line charged with making sure the line doesn't stop that is that the moving belt doesn't stop one pair stands with their legs spread apart facing each other and you unload the flats of empty bottle containers the ones you see going by on the back of trucks in the street those long trucks the truck pulls up from the distribution point full of flats with empty bottles and the empties team unloads it and places the boxes on the up belt which takes them on to the bottle-washing machine when the flat is empty the other team starts in with the flats

103

of full bottles that come up on the other belt when the flat is full the fork lift with its two long teeth comes along and puts it up on the truck which then goes out to the distribution points when you tell it like this it sounds real easy ratty rat friend the real thing is to be there tossing empty boxes on the belt for a half hour and then in the next half hour putting full boxes on the flat making sure they're on right and the team that worked before with the fulls that's how you say it are off to take a half hour break at the window where the bottles on their way to the washing machine go by you have to check to make sure they are capless and there's nothing in them that the washing process can't take care of like rocks or paint or tar from the window you move to the opening that's what it's called and the same thing all over again ratty rat friend it sounds easy but by the time you are in the second round you feel the back pain getting worse the boxes slip out of your hands when you try to grab them because you've got to pick up two at a time if they are the big ones the secret lies in a brief abrupt effort make the box fly and you handle it in the air as though it were a piece of paper and calculate well where you want it to come down there's got to be a rhythm you figure you'll lose four to six pounds a day it would do you good you're so chunky you must eat like mad and I'm almost out of wine no matter I almost can't feel the headache anymore just a pleasant throbbing when you see the full boxes coming with the necks of the bottles sticking out you say here come the Chinamen because truth is they all look alike and they come marching up with no stopping them no matter how tired you are you've got to keep on because the boxes can pile up and then the belt stops and when the belt stops the whole line stops the washing machine stops the dirty window operation stops and the clean window operation stops those guys are the real dudes the ones who more than ten years before started out tossing boxes and are now in the back that's what you say in the back to describe the ones who only have to sit and watch the full bottles go by in case the dirty window operator maybe let a dirty bottle get by and the washing machine didn't get it clean and the ones working the filling machine didn't see it and so the dirty bottle would get smuggled by and sometime in a bar when they serve you a bottle with hairs or bits of cork in it it's because those in charge of clean bottle exam were sleeping and they fall asleep not because they are sleepy but because if you had to look at bottles marching by in front of your eyes you would fall asleep hypnotized too you *get it ratty rat friend now go on and tell one of the guys back there to get working even if it's only a half hour loading cases they give you hell they know what it's like to heave boxes they pretend they forgot when they joke with the new guys as if they had started out working on a job sitting down but they sure remember how their back would hurt them and they would go to the company doctor whose only job is to tell them to be back on the job in the morning and he gives you just an aspirin of course if you make a fuss the doctor will shine some lights on you and that relieves the pain somewhat you've got to put up with this during the entire first season it's a little easier during the second one during the season three shifts are working round the clock the machines never stop one week you go in the morning the next week in the afternoon and the third week at night you never get any decent sleep just when you're used to sleeping in the morning you get the next shift and you have to go back sleeping nights but it all works out if you can stand it at first it gets better after that because you become a robot a machine that only thinks about overtime and while the sweat is dripping off your forehead and clouding your eyes and your whole body is dripping wet as though you'd been out in the rain you are only adding up in your head how much you're making that month how much for the night shift how much for not missing any days how much for your output how much as a bonus and how much for overtime on various shifts because night overtime is one thing and morning overtime something else and there are a lot of guys who ask to work only at night while their wives sleep holding the pillow at least that's what they hope right ratty rat friend what I can't hear you oh that's fine then I don't want to wake you up the thing is that it is embarrassing to have to put up with the bosses and smile at them so they'll pick you when there are no overtime hours it's ugly for everyone believe what I'm telling you I wouldn't lie The Duke doesn't lie and certainly not to you ratty rat friend and if living went up in price every year we asked for a raise it was a ritual you worked listlessly for two days the machines broke down and suddenly the raise would come through it was never what we asked for but something was better than nothing you had to put a lock on your locker otherwise they would steal even the hanger once one of the delegates was the victim of a big robbery imagine that ratty rat friend to have the guts to rob one of the delegates the delegate general came by and spoke to each of the shifts while we were* eating and said that if we wanted to steal one of the machines I'll help you myself but not a fellow worker you don't rob a buddy and we all clapped but the thief never turned up if they had ever gotten ahold of him I pity the poor guy not even the board of directors could have saved him during our breaks we all went into the bathroom it was the only place to go and we would sit around and smoke and drink pop right ratty rat friend you know how you drink pop you take the cap off you cover the top with your thumb and you shake it well and then you take your thumb off you repeat this several times until all the gas is gone the gas is bad because it increases your heartbeat and ferments your food in the stomach that's what everybody said there and you know how those who work in something are the ones who know all about it what the doctors say that it helps to digest your food is a lie believe me I'm not lying you've got The Duke's word you have no idea how humiliating it is to be frisked everytime you leave the job just like you were I don't know what if someone is going to steal he doesn't work a job right that's clear as crystal don't you think so ratty rat friend it's as though the thief who goes into a bank to rob it were told fine but go work one of the windows first the pain has come back in my forehead it isn't much I'll drink up what's left that'll calm me down so I can carry out the job right ratty rat friend you want a drink look it's your last chance okay if you don't want one it's your business don't say I didn't ask Don José offered me a cigarette first and when he saw my bag he thought I was on my way to train at some club that I was an athlete that I was into some sport hah I don't play sports I told him I'm on my way home from the plant and I have some clothes in the bag and I use it to carry sandwiches the pop is free for us and I smiled real pleased at him afterwards we would see each other now and then

Sorel, Walter *and* The Duke *are strolling leisurely through the Zoo. School children dressed in white uniforms cross their path. The animals in their cages contemplate the strollers with Olympic indifference.* Sorel *wants to get it straight.*

'. . . Keep in mind that I deliver what I promise. Besides, if you are not on my side, you are against me . . .'

'You're certain that the dollars are OK?'

'That's a dumb question.'

'And Don Jorge?'

'After a month or two, he won't even remember it. It's simply a question of taking care of yourself in these times. What do you say, Duke?'

'Count me in.'

'Me, too. But where are the dollars?'

'That's my insurance.'

Sorel *notices a strange hand movement* Walter *makes. Suddenly, two men appear. One with a bow-tie. He tries to make eye contact with* The Duke. *He realizes he has been betrayed.*

'I would never have thought it from you guys.'

'Don Jorge said the same thing about you . . .'

They walk toward the exit. Suddenly, Sorel *jumps on a moving merry-go-round. Suddenly everybody is running in and out among the children. Their guns flash in the open.* Sorel *is faster and eliminates one of them. He runs into the lions' pavilion, and the roaring together with the gunshots produce an exaggerated echo. The chase continues in the open before the shock of the people walking by. A woman falls wounded and the panic becomes general. Everybody tries to take cover behind the trees or falls to the ground.* Sorel *runs desperately toward the exit. One of the keepers is closing the gate.* Sorel *shoots at him and the man falls down, leaving the gate open. The gunman with the bow-tie succeeds in wounding him in the chest.* Sorel *falls. The other is about to finish him off when* The Duke *shoots him.* The Duke *goes over to* Sorel, *helps him to his feet. Fending off* Walter's *attack, they make it out of the Zoo and reach the car.* Sorel *is badly hurt, and* The Duke *drives off in a hurry.* Walter *climbs into his car and pursues them. They follow paths that wind through the woods, missing cars coming in the opposite direction. They are going the wrong way. They leave the road, they come back onto it. The bouncing around of the car is rough on* Sorel, *but the fresh air coming in through the window keeps him from passing out despite the pain in his chest and the blood that is soaking his shirt. He looks at* The Duke *driving with a sure hand.*

'Thanks. But why did you do it? . . .'

'I don't know. I haven't the faintest idea. Maybe just the need for a change of pace . . .'

The car weaves dangerously between two trucks. It's a bit banged up but it gets through. But Walter *has crashed head-on going almost 120 miles an hour.*

The Duke *feels a pressure in his right arm.* Sorel, *with his eyes wide open, is holding a paper toward him. He takes it and leaves the roadway, turning the car into the woods.*

'At the airport, at the International Hotel . . . the dollars are there . . . in suitcases. Enjoy them. I told them I would come for them within a week . . . to pick up the briefcase. "And they lit a fire where they came together, and the flame burned the wicked." Hah . . .'

'It would be better to take them to Don Jorge. First we'll see a doctor, someone I know.'

The car stops in the middle of an open area. He no longer feels the pressure on his arm. Sorel's *eyes are open, but they no longer see a thing. Blood continues to drip down his clothes, reaching the upper part of his pants. His white shirt, with bright red stains, is wrinkled into an irregular pattern. His open mouth shows not the slightest tremor of the lips. The furrows have disappeared from his* *forehead. The shadow of the trees. The singing of the birds flying* *after one another. Silence. Light filters through the leaves. Quiet.* The Duke *rests his forehead on the steering wheel. He doesn't* *know what to do. He would like to explain his actions to himself.* *Why did he help* Sorel? *Was it worth it? He looks again at the* *body. So much running around, so much fighting, just for this?* *For the first time he has a sense of death. Now that the one who did* *all the thinking for him no longer existed. There was a sharp* *buzzing in his ears, preventing him from seeing clearly. How to* *explain to himself the inexplicable. He must have completed one* *stage, just like finishing a round. You sit down on the little stool* *and ask yourself, what round is this? Then you space out the fight.* *And what round is it that's just over? Is the fight almost over? Or* *has it finished?* Sorel *is the irrefutable proof that something has* *ended. He'll never call him again. They'll never do jobs together* *again.* Walter *neither. It's not likely he made it either.* The Duke *realizes his solitude. During a quiet afternoon. The blood is* *getting the seat all dirty. He pulls the body out and drags it over* *among some trees. He checks the pockets. He keeps the money* *and buries the documents some distance away. He pulls some* *branches off and covers* Sorel's *body. He gets into the car. Time* *passes. He digs the documents up. He cleans the passport off.* Sorel *and he were about the same age. With the same features. The* *same hair. The photograph is rather old. He could easily be* Sorel. *He puts the passport in his pocket. Along with the stub for the* *luggage. He takes his seat at the steering wheel and thinks.*

He had met Don Jorge while he was a doorman at the Niagara. Champ, there are better things in store for you is what he said, someone who set the crowds to roaring can't be a simple doorman. And the next day he went to Don Jorge's fabulous office, scared, not knowing what to ask for or why he'd gone. Perhaps just to get out of a rut. He always did pat him on the back and call him Champ. At first he would answer timidly that he'd never been a champion, that unfortunately he had lost in a dramatic fight and that he hadn't been able to get a rematch, nor ever fight again because in that fight he'd ended up with a detached retina. But after a while he got used to being called Champ, after all . . .

At first he only drove Don Jorge's car. Then he drove the car for the ones who did the jobs. Until one night he held the gun. From then to pulling the trigger was a flick of the finger. Drink is necessary, it helps you to believe that everything will go away fast. Before going to bed you've got to say: It's all a nightmare and tomorrow it will all be gone. With time some doors are shut, and you've got no choice but to take advantage of the ones that open up. You walk right on in and that's that. And now there's no getting out. All because he believed in Don Jorge. Who would have ever believed that such an old fellow could be involved in this at his age? Everybody always admired him. He knew how to be open and to say things to your face. To stand up to the toughest of the lot and bow him down with only a look. That's how he had dominated him. The best thing about him was that he never held grudges. For example, when the Pole played that dirty trick on him, his first reaction was to promise to string him up by the balls, but he soon got over it. He never even batted an eye when they later told him that the Pole was in Panama. Let him be, he said, after all you've got to give him credit for nerve. What can have become of the Pole? Is he still in the white slave trade? He was very intelligent. He's probably in Europe or the United States. How much money is in the briefcase? A lot, quite a lot. Otherwise Sorel wouldn't have taken the chance. How can I lose? If it's too big an amount, let them come looking for me. What the Pole got was quite a bit. The worst that could happen is that they will kill me. And, then? I'm old enough to die. The rest of my life is not going to be very happy, anyway. What kind of change could take place? No chance of any change of scenery. What, then? I'm not about to become a priest. It all depends on how Don Jorge takes it. When he forgave the Pole it was because his deals were going great guns and the operation suited him fine. On the other hand, he'll blow Newman away when he gets his hands on him. Sure, that's a totally different rivalry. There's too much hate between them. If he got rid of the girls it was because there was no other way to handle it. It just depends on what mood he's in. He'll really be surprised about me. At first he won't believe it. He always believed I lacked initiative. Fine, it's never too late to start. Even if it's to show he's wrong to think he has everybody all sized up and knows who will do what and who won't. Just to confuse him. He'll shut himself up for a week.

Bring him to me alive, he'll yell before shutting the door. But he was always good to me. Always. So, then why am I going to betray him? Why? Just to know if I've got the guts? Maybe. For a change of pace. To keep on fighting. So as not to repeat my daily death. If I don't do it now I never will. I will grow old and go back to work as a doorman. Putting up with jerks all over again who remember my fights better than I do. Smile at them when I want them to drop dead. When you get right down to it, I don't owe him a thing. I worked a long time for him and did a good job. I could hide out a few days at Doña Lola's. None of the guys knew about that place. I can wait four days, better five, that way it'll be Wednesday, the middle of the week. I can get the briefcase at night under whatever pretext. At worst, I'll just have to knock the watchman over the head. And instead of getting away by plane, I can backtrack and use the Wop's motorboat. Once across the river it'll be easier to get away. So it's all set. After all, I'm old enough to die.

He turned the headlights on and the starting of the motor broke the silence of the forest.

. . . That play from the waist was just great. Not only did he come out swinging, but he dodged all of the blows from his opponent. He was a born boxer! A real one. He had class, charm, courage. There's no doubt he'll be the best for a long time to come. But, and there's always a but, only in the ring. When he'd come down from the ring he was a real loser. Done? What's wrong with that one? Next time get a real cameraman and forget about the apprentices. Don't get all worked up, I only meant it as a joke. It's the speed that's not right . . . Okay, cut out the crap, you'll end up making me come out too fast and they'll think I'm a clown rather than a news reporter. As I was saying, he was a loser. By the way, don't pan in too close, it makes my jowl show. I've got to go on a diet. That's what a doctor told me. Well, that's what happens with age. Tell me when you've got the camera ready, okay? Don't try to film without letting me know or we'll all end up in jail! As I was saying, he was a loser. That's the right word. The very same woman he left when he started to earn big money and then tried to find again right away, it seems that she . . . Ah, so you know about that? And what did you ask her? She ran you off?! What a jerk you are. You can tell you haven't much experience in these things. When you have to interview women like that you have to give them all you got, even if it means sleeping with them. Then they'll tell you anything, they'll even recite the phone book to you backward. I'm really surprised. But that's okay . . . When I first started out I got burned a couple of times too. Well, it seems that the Mirna gal wasn't the only one supporting him. It seems that he had about ten women and a cheap dancer was in charge of them, she's somewhere in Central America now, he was deeply involved with her and then she up and left him for someone else. Don't think she was the first heavy-weight deal he was involved with. It's not that way, I know the real story. He came from that sort of background before he even met Don José. That's the straight truth. What would I be lying for?! You're the reporter and I'm just answering the questions . . . Okay, calm down, I'll stick to the sports story and nothing else. And the business about the kid . . . ? What do you mean what kid? His son! See how you don't have the real story? He had this kid with one of the women from his golden age, and it seems that she ditched him. Since he never trusted anyone, he was ready to believe that it was someone else's brat, and the kid got taken directly from the delivery room to the orphanage. See what animals we're dealing with?! . . . Yeh, okay. In any case, he was a delinquent, a loser. Just wait and see when the lid blows off and see how the whole mess smells. Why do you think Don José disappeared? He disappeared because he was a decent old duffer and when he saw that the guy was down the drain and couldn't be saved, he dropped out . . . Don't kid me. They all end up this way. They're all just cannon fodder. Look at it, now you want to defend him . . . Sure let's talk in impartial terms. He was an SOB. Of course he was! But look here, you're the only one talking. The problem is that you're new at the game, and you'll see when you get tired of pounding the typewriter. Fine, fine. But he was a delinquent. The lid's got to blow off, you'll see. I know of at least one for sure . . . The one he killed at the terminal. How can you deny that?! Even the school kids know about that one. Come off that stuff that he's innocent until proven guilty. We can't get anywhere with that line. Let me ask you the following. Why are you so hot on The Duke if you never saw him fight? Tell me that. Look at the last fight, the Tano killed him, made mincemeat out of him. Well, if he didn't fall down it was because he didn't fall down, the truth of the matter was that he looked worse than Frankenstein. And he killed him in the rematch too! Don't give me that about the eye, what got detached was his brain, yeh his brain came loose. Okay, it looks like they've got the camera set up. Are you ready, Fellini? Fine, yes I understand. Come on, I'm not retarded. When you signal with your arm I'll count to three and begin. Let's go. Don't come in close or I'll kill you! Yes, shsh, quiet. (One, two, three.) The entire country is in mourning: it has lost one of its favored sons . . .

of his eyes and he was foaming at the mouth he chased us for a block with the knife but the people going by didn't grasp what was going on or they thought we were escaping from a madhouse to withdraw is not to run away Miguel shouted and that's how I saved my first fight a fiasco I lost by quitting in the second round Don José put up with jokes from everybody but nevertheless I knew that I would end up in front and Don José knew it too he told me you did fine let's be more careful with your guard that rotten fight was a lot of good to me I swore by my mother that I would never fall down again and I kept my word my last fight damn it if it hadn't been for my eye I'm sure I would've won hell they took my permit away how exciting it was to hear the roar of the crowd I was the best attraction around newspapers and magazines used the largest letters possible to spell out The Duke I was the best no matter what they say time'll go by and they'll still remember me even my son where could he be it must be about ten years ago that Don José brought him to me from the home he got special permission I was embarrassed that after eight years I was seeing him for the first time because they all thought he had died here's your child I heard Don José's voice whisper in my ear I couldn't see him like I would have liked to embrace him ask his forgiveness but things that you can't do when you want to lose their importance in kind of a fog I saw a fine boy who had no idea why he was standing there in front of a dying man he looked at me without feeling his mother wasn't like that she had the prettiest eyes I ever saw and when she looked at you she laid your heart bare and that kid had no strength at all in his look I realized he was anxious to get out of there as soon as possible and leave that smelly hospital and that dying drunk who had been run over by a truck I heard Don José when he drew him close with an arm around his shoulders he said give him a kiss it's your father I'll never forgive Don José for that I wanted to say something to tell him to shut up for him to get that kid out of my ruined sight I saw the grimace on his face when he leaned over to kiss me on my bandages being careful not to kiss me on my face purple with iodine I couldn't move or talk I could barely manage a few tears of rage I had never been so miserable before in my life ah ratty rat friend what a punishment life is Mirna never knew about my son she came on the scene later she stood by me until we split during my years of splendor when The Duke was born when I would raise my arms and the roar of the crowd would shake the *stadium I had it all together I was elegant and aggressive just like that enemy commentator said who couldn't help but recognize that I was the best I had a lot of women around me during my splendor all of them great lookers but none of them worth a damn when I needed someone by my side she was the only one there without anyone having asked her to be she could pull money out of a hat to get me looking decent she was already working in the dives I never said a thing and she kept on working even when the going got easy you've got to look the other way she had lost color in her face and her features became more pronounced I continued to drink and smoke this is my last cigarette ah ratty rat friend where are all my friends because I had a lot of friends they helped me out I've got to make a list and send them a thankyou letter I've got to do it before my memory starts to fail me before I die in Niagara I met Don José and I got into the game without even thinking at first it was only easy ones then they used my fists to get information out of their rivals and wine helps you forget what you're doing it's just like bringing down that long hammer on the center of the cow's head who moans moans moo moo moo and you bring the hammer down again until they drop it would be better to get it right the first time with a single shot you aim the barrel between the horns and pull the trigger the bullet does its job kill and the cow falls in a heap without a single moan ah ratty rat friend today's my day to win I swear word of the The Duke my first death was legal I couldn't stop hitting besides when you aren't careful a death blow can come along they're fatal and ruin everything I had sworn never to fall again and I kept my word I lost sometimes but they never counted to ten on me never instead I made more than one guy kiss the mat I swear I didn't mean to kill him I only wanted him to fall for him to lie down and rest a bit because I was all worn out too and the sweat was running in my eyes and I couldn't see I struck the hulk struck to kill but it was his fault for not giving up sure I struck to kill but I didn't want to kill him ay ratty rat friend hey where are you going wait the best part is still to come be good don't leave me you'll make me lucky and today my luck'll change careful don't fall fine best of luck to you we'll meet again somewhere on the road of life so long friend today my luck's going to change I swear it you got The Duke's word on it there must be more to life than this there's got to be something more . . .*

The fire enveloped a large area of shacks. The firemen took drastic measures with others, tearing them down in an attempt to keep the fire from spreading and the destruction from being any greater.

While the firemen moved about doing their job, a rumor began to spread. The fire had got its start in a certain shack, specifically, in a hideout. The police were on their way.

One of the firemen walked up to another one and said:

'Do you know what people are saying? That there was a gunman in the shack where the fire started, someone who used to be a famous boxer.'

Diego clenched his teeth. He had a strong urge to throw down the fire hose and go over to the shack, but he resisted it. He called to someone to come and take his place. There wasn't much to be done, just wait. Unfortunately, the rain had stopped. Perhaps if it had continued for a while longer, this fire wouldn't have started. He went over to the shack. Some of the wood and the siding were still hot and smoldering. He hacked his way through with his hatchet. He prayed to God that his premonition of the truth would be wrong. Just as he was knocking over some slats, he heard the siren of the squad car. The open siding allowed him to see a burned body, the face formless but still giving off some whitish wisps. The flesh was taut, the eyes open, and one of the arms was rigid and extended. Perhaps many would doubt the identity of this body, but not him. Even though it was burned and in that position, it had the aura of The Duke. The hot air hurt his eyes and he couldn't hold the tears back. As he withdrew to make room for the police, he thought about the newspaper headlines and about the album that he kept in a box beneath his dresser. He pressed his thumb and index finger lightly against his eyes to ease his distress and swore firmly that he would add no further clipping to it.